SHOTGUN, LIES & ALIBIS

A COZY MOUNTAIN TOWN MYSTERY - 1

TRENA REDDING

1

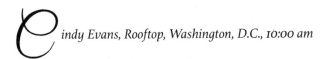

indy Evans, Rooftop, Washington, D.C., 10:00 am

How did I get myself into this mess?

I mean, sure, working for the DEA sounds exciting on paper, but when you're perched on top of a six-story building in the middle of Washington D.C., sweating like a sinner in church and trying not to shake like a leaf, it's not exactly a walk in the park. But hey, at least I had my trusty Remington seven hundred three-o-eight and my range bag to keep me company.

As I settled into my sniping position, I couldn't help but think about how Agent Michaelson was doing, posing as an undercover food vendor, and Agent Nichols, dressed as a sandwich delivery guy, perched on a road bike around the corner. Talk about commitment to the role.

I focused on the revolving doors of the building across the street, and let out a sigh as the target, an associate of a known drug dealer, came into view. Pushing a hand truck stacked with boxes, he strolled right up to the front door of a public building like he owned the place. Talk about chutzpah.

As I prepared to take the shot, I couldn't help but think that this Abdul guy and his crew had been getting away with their dirty dealings for far too long. But little did they know, they were about to have a run-in with the DEA's finest.

Just as I was about to pull the trigger, Agent Nichols rode around the corner and straight into my target, causing him to drop the boxes and start shouting profanity. I fired a shot, but it missed by a hair and hit a brick, causing a cloud of dust. I fired again, but the target wisely crawled behind the fallen boxes for cover.

Just as I was about to pat myself on the back for a job well done, I heard someone approaching. I quickly aimed my rifle and prepared for the worst, only to find Deputy Cunningham poking his head out from behind a door. "Shoot me and you'll have a lot of explaining to do to Director Sanchez," he called out.

Frustrated, I put down my weapon. "You will have to explain why you snuck up on the department's best sharp-shooter in the middle of a mission. What are you doing here?" I asked.

"You took the shot," Cunningham replied.

"I am aware of that," I defended.

"Your mission was to provide cover, not kill anyone," Cunningham insisted.

"He reached for his piece," I protested.

"The guy went for his phone. You misread the situation." *Phone? Oh boy, this is gonna be one for the books.*

Cunningham stepped forward. "Director Sanchez sent me to get you. We have new intel on the latest shipment of blow. Our plan is to intercept the shipment before the buyer gets his hands on it. Pack your stuff. The director wants us to roll in like a wrecking ball and take them by surprise. And hopefully, this time I won't have to remind you to check your target before you shoot."

I couldn't help but let out a chuckle. "Looks like I'm about to be a one-woman wrecking ball. Let's do this."

With Cunningham in the lead, I arrived at the armored, black SUV parked two blocks away. Since I didn't like to put my equipment in the cargo area unless completely necessary, I placed my gear in the back seat next to me. I never wanted to be left unprepared for a surprise guest. Armored, black SUVs had a reputation of carrying someone important. Someone hard criminals might want to ransom. Or kill. Or both.

Deputy Cunningham sat next to my bag and instructed Executive Assistant Rachel Roos to start driving.

Rachel looked at me in the rearview mirror. "You look like a Holly Bush," she said. I rolled my eyes and very maturely stuck my tongue out at her.

Rachel, a sassy brunette who stood about five-foot-eight and smelled of lilacs, made me look like a female roughneck in my camouflage gear. She looked innocent as she perched clacking her nails on the leather armrest, but we all knew to give her respect for being a badass. She proved her skills on more than one occasion.

"Very funny, Rachel. I've heard all the redhead and curly hair jokes out there. Yours is only slightly clever," I quipped.

Rachel steered the SUV onto the road. "The director wants you in his office within the hour. What did you do this time, Evans?"

Rachel rarely passed up an opportunity to tease me. Only slightly irritated by her question, I shifted away from Cunningham and discretely flipped her the bird in the mirror. I paused and composed myself before answering.

"My assignment was to provide cover and that's what I did. I swear I saw a weapon."

"Well, you shot prematurely and almost killed Fahid, Abdul's brother," Cunningham chided. "The screw-up guarantees that you become a target for lots of bad people."

Cunningham didn't ramble on, but he didn't need to. I had made a mistake. I hated making errors.

My frustration mounted as the reality of disappointing Cunningham, and worse, Director Sanchez, soaked into my bloodstream like chilled sludge. Although Director Sanchez, a sixty-two-year-old agent who worked for the agency for forty years, had a mean streak, I still cared about his opinion of my work.

"I came to pull you off that roof because we believe we have an informant in our office." Cunningham's voice increased in volume as the sound of the SUV's engine got louder. "Somehow, Fahid found out you are on Abdul's tail, and put the word out. He has every thug, arms dealer, and drug lord looking for you. They are circulating your photo and offering five hundred thousand bounty for your head. You, officially, have become their primary target. Especially now that you took a shot at him."

Worse news. The chill I'd been feeling turned to ice, and I rubbed my arms against the cold.

Even Roos gave me a sympathetic glance in the rearview mirror.

If I stayed in this city, I was dead.

Nothing I could do about the leak in our office. The poor judgement call, however, seemed a much safer thing to focus on. "Listen. Random, unexpected events happen. No way could I have known he was reaching for a phone. I only had a fraction of a second to make a decision."

Cunningham crossed his arms, the smell of Old Spice deodorant filled the inside of the vehicle. "May I remind you that you used the "random, unexpected events" excuse when you blew up a boat carrying meth to the Inner Harbor? Your task involved recovering the shipment, intact. Multiple people swamped the area. If you weren't such a good swimmer, you could have drawn a lot of attention to yourself."

I couldn't believe he was bringing that up... again. "The ship should have been carrying crank only. You expected me to know they got a deal on C-4, as well? Your informant didn't even know until after the Coast Guard found evidence during their investigation. The timeline left very little time for reconnaissance."

Cunningham scoffed. "This is what I am telling you, Evans. You go off halfcocked sometimes, without thinking things through."

The doors of the SUV closed in on me, trapping me like a dog being kenneled. I needed to plan my escape. The heat generated under the clothes I wore, irritated my skin, adding to my frustration. "I'm passionate about my work. I see the big picture first, which might mean I miss a few details," I said with a sigh and a shrug.

Cunningham checked his phone and shifted in his seat. "A few expensive details. But it seems plans have changed. After we meet with the director, I'm taking you to your place to pack a bag. You're going underground until we can clean up this mess."

My gut clenched. "What? Where? Just reassign me. Don't make me crawl into a hole and hide. Paris? Berlin? I'll brush up on my Russian, and you can send me into Ukraine."

"Half a million," Cunningham responded, his eyebrows raised as he leaned forward. "Did you hear me?"

"I heard you," I said, leaning back and resting my head against the seat. That kind of money would attract the attention of professionals from all over the world. I wouldn't be safe until the contract offer was cancelled. Which meant Abdul and his people would have to be dead. "This could take months."

Cunningham exhaled. "So, you were listening."

"Where am I going?" I asked, bracing myself for the answer.

"You are headed to good ol' colorful Colorado," Cunningham said with a chuckle.

My knowledge of the state being limited, I searched my brain for a viable argument. "Colorado? I've been downgraded to chasing pot dealers? Haven't you heard; weed is legal in Colorado. Everyone smokes pot just because they can. Eighty-five-year-old grandmas hit the pot shops daily since no law exists against getting the drug anymore. What, exactly, will I do in Colorado, rustle cattle?"

Roos briefly looked over her shoulder from the driver's seat. "You'll work as a home health physical therapist and get to know the people in the area. Small mountain town. Isolated."

"I haven't done physical therapy work for years. I am not even sure I remember how. Also, I am not licensed to practice in Colorado."

As a teen, I spent many years taking care of my mom, who eventually died from cancer at the young age of forty-two. I never intended to follow the path of helping people with their physical ailments the rest of my life. However, I worked hard in college and graduate school and became a physical therapist in my twenties. One day, after work, I was approached by a man from the agency and asked to join. I liked working as a physical therapist, but protecting our country from drug lords and gangs fit my temperament better than working as a caregiver. So, I said yes.

The idea of working again as a therapist, teaching people how to walk and listening to them complain about their pain daily, made me feel desperate and nauseous. The smell of exhaust from the diesel truck in front of us coming through the air conditioning vents didn't help.

Cunningham crossed his arms on his chest. "We set up a license for you in the state and took care of the continuing education requirements. Get comfortable with the idea. You might be there a while. Several months could pass before we straighten this mess out."

I groaned, "It's like my own personal cozy mystery. I have to solve the case of my own identity while pretending to be a physical therapist in small town Colorado. I hope there's a cute sheriff to help me along the way."

Cunningham just shook his head, "Just focus on staying alive, Evans."

Rachel chimed in, "Don't worry, Evans. I'm sure you'll find some excitement in a small town. Maybe a missing cat or a case of apple pie theft."

"Great. Just great," I grumbled. "I'm going to a small town to chat up the locals and stay out of everyone's way. It's like being sent to small town jail. But instead of a cell, I get to be a physical therapist to the elderly. My skills as a DEA agent are going to waste, chasing after grannies with walkers instead of drug dealers with guns."

We arrived at Director Sanchez's office faster than I hoped we would.

He sat behind his giant mahogany desk, with an over-sized mug displaying a picture of his daughter and wife on a Bahamas trip. File folders from various cases littered the top of his desk. He didn't look up immediately.

I took the reaction to be a bad sign. My anxiety increased by the second. I figured I would go into self-preservation mode before he had a chance to shoot me down. A good butt-chewing usually transpired during these types of situations.

Waiting until he looked up, I launched my defense. "Good morning, sir. With all due respect, may I suggest you keep me in the city, where my skills as an agent would provide the most benefit to the department? You know I am the best person for the job. I have been working on this case for over a year."

Director Sanchez set his mug down, the sound like a gavel on wood.

He leaned forward on the desk. "Your mission was to make sure no other agents or civilians were hurt. Instead, you drew attention to them on one of the busiest streets in D.C. Plus, we detected movement from this drug ring and have determined the safest move is to get you out of the area. Abdul wants you eliminated. You're hurting his operation. He has too many players in place, and you're making him pull in extra resources."

Disappointment settled in at the thought of screwing up another assignment. "I'm doing my job, sir."

"Nice work, Evans. Until today, that is. Nichols is taking over your case. We already have a job lined up with Mountain Tops Home Health Agency. You start on Monday."

My shoulders slouched as I realized the consequences of my mistake. Worse yet. I deserved the punishment. "You're putting me in the mountains? But, sir, you know I'm a city girl. I'm liable to die from boredom. Colorado has nothing to do but ski, bike, and sit around a fire. I'm really more of a city girl," I responded, trying to lighten the mood.

Cunningham gave me a wry smile. "Listen, Evans. The people there are too busy struggling to breathe the thin air and make their brains work at the same time. Crime there involves things like catching too many fish or trespassing on private property. It'll be a cakewalk."

I rolled my eyes. "Cakewalk? More like a death march. I'll be stuck in the mountains, surrounded by snow and pine trees, and all I'll have to keep me company is my trusty hot water bottle. But I suppose it's better than being hunted by Abdul and his goons. I'll make the best of it, but I'll be counting the days until I can come back to the city and get back to doing what I do best: busting dirtbags."

Colorado might be known for its mountains and outdoor activities, but you can be damn sure I'll keep my sharpshooter skills sharp, just in case Abdul and his crew decide to make an appearance in this darling mountain town. Who knows, maybe I'll even pick up a new hobby like knitting or bird-watching. But make no mistake, I'll be ready for action if and when the time comes.

I turned to leave the room, my mind already working on a plan to take down Abdul and clear my name. One thing was for sure, I was not going to let a little thing like being exiled to the mountains stop me from doing my job and keeping our country safe.

*a*s Agent Roos drove me to the airport in the black SUV, I couldn't help but feel like I was in a spy movie. She reached over the seat and handed me two phones, one black and one silver. "The black one is for use as a business phone and the silver one is a burner," she said, "anyone from the agency who needs to talk to you will call you on the burner phone."

I decided to use the burner phone to call my dad and warn him about my sudden departure. "Hey, Dad. It's Cindy," I said as he answered on the second ring.

"What did you do this time honey, steal the Mona Lisa or something?" He chuckled.

I tried to explain the situation to him, "I got pulled from a mission and now I'm being sent to Colorado to lay low. Director Sanchez says I'm now a target."

"Well, at least that means they know you're good at your job." He laughed.

I longed for a different solution but I knew my dad would always support me. "You know I'm the best shooter they have." I bit off the tip of a fingernail.

"Which is exactly why they need to protect you. You're an asset they can't afford to lose. Keep in touch our usual way. I need to know you're safe."

Throughout the flight, thoughts swarmed my brain, roiling my belly like a bunch of agitated bees. I couldn't wrap my head around the idea of doing physical therapy again... uggh! The nervousness settled into a tight ball in my stomach and, mixed with the greasy smell of another passenger's fast food making me nauseous. I leaned my seat back as far as it would go and closed my eyes. Over and over in my mind, I replayed the situation on the rooftop but couldn't figure out how Abdul's people identified me. I swapped my burner phones frequently so they couldn't have tracked me through my cell. Who could have tipped him off, and why?

After hours of flying, I still had no answers as we landed in Denver International Airport. I still had another flight to take to get to the Rocky Mountains. The only one available looked like a death trap. The aircraft accommodated ten passengers and was probably used as a crop duster when the rickety thing wasn't flying people. And when we started down the runway, the whole thing creaked and moaned, tilting from side to side like a backyard chicken running at full speed.

Once the aircraft ascended into the air, I took a deep breath and fought for calm until I heard the cry of a small boy in the middle of the plane. Apparently, he had the same feelings about the wild ride because he vomited in the aisle. The foul, sour smell hit my nose and turned my stomach. His parents cleaned off his mouth and clothes, while I held my breath, hoping to avoid breathing again until we landed. I did not have any idea of how to deal with crying kids, so I kept to myself and wondered again about how I ended up in this mess. Then, I remembered I was now being hunted by a group of very unwavering killers. I sat back and closed my eyes, deciding a screaming kid and a pile of vomit was better than being dead. Still, I hoped the torture would be over soon.

At the baggage claim, I retrieved my hard-shelled suitcase with my personal items and my trusty unloaded weapon inside. My eyes scanned the lock to ensure the mechanism remained intact. I was ready for anything, except maybe an hour-long taxi ride to my destination.

The taxi driver peered in the rearview mirror. "I hope you have a tough stomach. The roads in this area wind back and forth so much you'll feel like I'm trying to give you a Swedish massage."

I smiled. "It's all right. It can't be much worse than that toy plane I took to get here." I couldn't help but notice all of the trucks and SUVs on the road. One of the trucks, being driven by a woman, had a sticker in the back window which read, *You silly rabbit. Trucks are for girls.*

Talk about being out of my element. I grew up riding the Metro in D.C.

The ride involved driving through some beautiful scenery which bordered the large Colorado River. Rushing water crashed into huge boulders, sending a spray of mist into the air. Winding back and forth on the interstate, next to the rapids, made me grab for the door handle and the edge of my seat. The dangerous roller coaster ride didn't seem to affect the driver as he appeared unbothered by putting our lives at risk.

Just in case the driver made an unfortunate mistake and veered off the edge of the cliff and down into the river, I calculated my escape plan from the taxi.

Thankfully, the car finally pulled off of exit twenty-four towards a town called Shotgun.

Shotgun, Colorado.

Yee-ha. I was hiding out here trying not to get shot and killed. The irony of the town's name did not go unnoticed.

The house Roos chose looked like an old log cabin which sat at the edge of the Colorado River. The cabin had a long gravel driveway with a pink flamingo lawn ornament at the entrance and a white SUV parked near the house. In the front of the home, a small, wooden porch with two rope hammocks hung from the roof. In the back, the property had a faded redwood deck with some "well-used" furniture and a small, glass table with four chairs. The view looked stunning, even to a city girl. Mountains spread across the entire horizon, with large, fluffy storm clouds overhead mixed with large patches of blue sky.

Three large hawks flew in the distance, circling the tip of one of the mountains. They made a loud, shrill *kee-ee* sound as they floated through the air.

I understood why someone would want to live here, especially after they retired. I didn't think, however, I could ever be such a person. The city and all of its charm were deeply embedded in my soul. Quiet, rural areas made me antsy.

Walking off the deck, I saw a fire pit surrounded by aging, plastic lawn chairs. A path led to the edge of the river with more of the same furniture and a few fishing poles standing on their ends. Standing still for a moment, I listened to the sound of rushing water, my muscles loosening as stress drained from my body. A cool mist tickled my face. I crouched to feel the temperature of the water. The cold water numbed my hand within seconds. I wouldn't be swimming in the river any time soon.

Hearing my stomach growl, I realized I hadn't eaten anything all day except for the breakfast burrito I bought from a roadside stand on my way to the office. The owner of the property had left the front door unlocked so I could get in. I walked inside the house and found a stone key holder with an etched mountain scene just inside the door. A sticky note hung on the side listing the user ID and password for the internet and the residence's mailing address. The owner was well prepared for a renter.

Grabbing a set of car keys, I jumped in the white SUV sitting in the driveway. My plan involved driving around the area to familiarize myself with my surroundings and to find some food. It was time to explore my new home, Shotgun, Colorado. And maybe, just maybe, I'll find a clue that will help me solve the mystery of why I was sent here in the first place.

Across the interstate, Grocer's Market sat next to a small strip of stores and restaurants. In the parking lot, the aptly named Evergreen Bank flashed lights claiming to be closed. I felt like I was in a different country, or maybe a different decade. Retail businesses were scattered along a single road leading through town. The local hot spots included a McDonald's, a Subway sandwich shop, and a few small, private restaurants.

Clearly, I would need to get better at home cooking, or maybe just invest in a good takeout app.

Other than a few gas stations, two hair salons, a small karate dojo, and a taxidermy shop with a sign stating *You shoot 'em, we stuff 'em*, no other retail businesses existed on the main street. Shotgun had a small county library, which seemed fairly busy. At the other end of town, a sketchy looking bar, called The Burning Mountain Saloon, sat up against the base of the mountain. Through the open front door, I saw two pool tables which looked like they had seen some rough nights.

Stopping at the Grocers Market, I searched for food and supplies. I must have arrived during the town social hour, since I had to bob and weave around small groups of people talking.

Blocking the path to the cucumbers, two guys dressed in bike jerseys, shorts that looked like they were wearing diapers, and clunky shoes talked about their latest adventure.

"Did you hit that single track trail I told you about on Canyon Road?"

"Nah, dude. My wife needed a break from the kids so I didn't have time. I'm just riding local today. I'll hit that this weekend, if she lets me."

"I know the feeling. Speaking of which, I better get home before Heather texts me with more stops to make. Catch ya later."

After finishing at the grocery store, I walked down to the liquor store to buy a bottle of Cabernet and found a long line of people at the cash register. Most had on uniforms or wore dirty, heavy-duty clothes like they had just gotten off work. I squeezed past the line, almost knocking down a stack of boxed wine displayed on a table in the middle of the small walkway. I made my selection quickly, eager to escape from the tight, narrow space as fast as possible.

The cashier, a middle-aged, overweight female with a grey, seventies hairstyle, smiled briefly. "How's it going?"

I placed the wine bottle on the crowded counter. "I think it'll take a while to adjust to the weather here." I rubbed my bare arms, warming myself. "Once the sun went behind the mountain, the temperature dropped shockingly fast."

She laughed. "We always say, if you don't like the weather in Colorado, wait five minutes. You'll learn really fast to dress in layers. If you do, you are prepared no matter what temperature is. The change is more drastic in the first few months of summer. It gets better in July and August."

I thanked her for the advice and as I walked out the door, I collided with a large, pot-bellied man. My eyes scanned him head to toe, taking in his size, posture and facial expression. *Definitely not agile enough to keep up with my skills.*

"Oh. Sorry about that. I wasn't even looking where I was going," he said. "Let me apologize." He widened his arms and embraced me in a bear hug then turned to go into the liquor store.

I couldn't help but laugh at the absurdity of the situation and thought to myself, maybe this cozy little town won't be so bad after all.

As he stepped inside, the cashier cried out, "Well, if it isn't Huggin' Harry!"

Well, that explains it. I giggled at the thought of the nickname they would bestow upon me eventually.

On my way home, in the middle of a circular road, stood a very large rock statue with hawks etched on one side, a guy riding a mountain bike on another, and a naked guy rock climbing. I laughed, thinking maybe the reason they made the road circular was so each person could view the naked guy from all sides. But then I wondered if it was a statue of the local nudist club president.

Apparently, the visual of the guy's butt cheeks showed too much for some of the locals because someone covered the offensive sight with an American flag bandana. I cringed at the thought of a group of people getting together to cover a statue's butt with a flag.

Finding my way back home was easy, since the area had only one major road in and out of the town. I made a mental note of this in case drug and arms dealers figured out my location, and I found myself on the run. I couldn't help but grin at the thought of being chased by a group of criminals in a small town like this.

Safely parked, I walked, grocery bags in hand, into my

rented cabin through the mudroom and into a living room with a gas stove. Beside the stove sat a small stack of firewood in an iron holder and several tools which looked like the previous owner might have been into medieval torture. I wondered how much practice would be needed to figure out how to light the stove, and if I would blow the place up in the process.

I decided on a meal which seemed symbolic of the area. The smell of sizzling steak and baked potato filled the house and made my mouth water. I poured myself a glass of wine and sat at my laptop to check my emails. I hoped to find out if Director Sanchez had come to his senses and sent me an email ordering me to return to D.C.

No such luck.

When we last talked, he didn't mention if I was allowed to contact him, Cunningham or Roos but said he would be in touch. I couldn't help but roll my eyes at the thought of Director Sanchez being a stick in the mud.

I wasn't holding my breath.

3

---

*A*fter chowing down on some grub, I hit the hay feeling like I could sleep for a hundred years. I left my window open to let in the fresh mountain air, filled with the delightful aroma of pine trees, oak brush, and a hint of skunk. In the city, I never left my window open at night because the smell of car exhaust and honking horns was enough to make a grown man cry. Plus, in the summer, my air conditioning bill would be higher than the national debt if I didn't keep my windows shut tight. But here in the mountains, the air coming through the window had me pulling the heavy comforter up to my chin. If this was summer, I was afraid to think about what winter would be like. Losing my toes to frostbite was definitely not on my bucket list.

I snuggled up with my trusty nine-millimeter under my pillow, feeling comforted by the fact that Cunningham let me bring my prized weapon. The rhythmic pulsing of blood in my ears kept time with my heartbeat. But then, all of a sudden, I heard an animal howling. My body tensed up as other creatures joined in, making an eerie chorus. Thankfully, the noises stopped, leaving just the sound of rushing water from the nearby river.

As I lay there trying to fall asleep, I couldn't help but think of the movie *My Cousin Vinny*. Joe Pesci's character struggled for days to get a good night's rest in Beecham County, Alabama because of the unfamiliar sounds of screeching animals. The first real night of sleep he got was when he was thrown in prison with constant fighting and other human noises at night. It reminded me that adjusting to my new living environment would take some time.

Just as I was about to drift off, something rustled the curtains of the window across the room. I quickly reached under my pillow to grab my nine-millimeter when something jumped onto my bed and brushed against my leg. Before I could turn and aim, I heard hissing, followed by a high-pitched growl. I did a roll and slid off the bed, launching across the room to turn on the light. As my eyes adjusted, I saw a puffy, black-and-white tail slide back out the window and disappear. I walked around the bed, sniffing my bedspread and pillows, hoping not to find the stench of skunk. Relieved when I smelled nothing out of the ordinary, I crawled back into bed. In the morning, I would figure out what type of animal had violated my space. I didn't want to make enemies by potentially shooting someone's pet.

The next morning, I woke up feeling like I had been hit by a truck. I spent the morning perusing patient files on the software that the home health company used for maintaining patient files. I reviewed all of the people I would be seeing in my first week. Each one had some detailed information of the individual, along with the previous therapist's notes. The process took me a long time because the internet moved at a snail's pace. Apparently, Wi-Fi signals did not travel very well through the mountains. I must have picked a popular time. I needed to figure out when the best time to get online would be so I could avoid the desire to throw my laptop into the river.

After organizing my schedule, I called each patient to introduce myself and arrange our appointment times. I also called the previous therapist to acquire information about the patients in order to make my transition a little less painful. She regaled me with quite a few interesting stories, letting me know I certainly wouldn't be bored.

With patients in order, I decided to do some research on the company, Mountain Tops Home Health Agency. The owner of the company, Dr. Ky Dalton, was the only M.D. in town and served as the family doctor, local surgeon, and coroner. The fact that he served in all three roles reminded me that Director Sanchez had truly removed me from the fast-paced life in Washington D.C. and put me in a slow-paced, simple town. I felt like I had been sent to adult detention. The home health agency served the Lower Fork Valley all the way from a town called Defiance to Shotgun. The job would require extensive driving time, but I was ready for the adventure.

When I felt ready to take on the week, I set out to figure out what type of animal had nearly become my bed buddy the night before. In the back of the property stood a rustic, wooden barn with uncovered windows and a partially collapsed roof. The building seemed like a perfect place for animals to hide during the day, so I cautiously swung open the barn door, ready to run if I saw a black butt with a white-and-black striped tail angled my direction. The barn smelled like a combination of rotting wood and musty, damp hay. Stepping inside, I nearly fell in a hole where the floor had rotted. In an attempt to recover my balance, I twisted my ankle, sending a sharp pain shooting up the side of my leg.

"Ya gotta be careful in these old barns. The change in the weather causes the boards to rot pretty easily," a young, male voice said from behind.

The hair on the back of my neck rose, and I whirled around. My visitor, a striking young man about six feet tall, most likely in his late teens, ranked low on my threat radar judging by his boyish face. He had a kind smile, wavy brown hair, and a thin frame. "I am looking for an animal that came through my bedroom window last night. I figured this would be a good place to start. And who are you?"

"Oh, sorry. My name is Bryce Riddle. I live over there," he said, pointing to a two-story, blue house about four hundred yards to the west. "My dad Joe is the county sheriff. Sometimes I get bored while he is working or when I'm not at school and hang out in this old barn. I didn't realize anyone new had moved in."

"I just got here. My name is Ally Justice." I held out my hand to shake. His grip was firm and strong. His handshake was the kind taught by someone in law enforcement or the military.

"Well, welcome to the neighborhood. We have quite a few creatures in this area that like to pay a visit. You get used to it," Bryce said, starting around the back of the barn.

I followed, tripping over old lawn mowers, shovels, and wheelbarrows along the way.

"So, what brought you to our humble mountain town?"

"I work as a physical therapist, and I got a call from a recruiter offering a job at Mountain Tops Home Health Agency. I've never lived anywhere but the city, so I figured the move would be an adventure," I lied smoothly, sticking my chest out, proud of how quickly I transitioned to an alias.

Bryce stopped and turned. "Oh. The business is owned by Dr. Dalton. My Grandma Helen is always trying to set him up with women in the area. She can't understand why a handsome, successful doctor is not already married. She does the same thing with my dad. You better watch out. She'll probably get to you next."

My heart sank as I imagined being set up on a date with the local doctor while trying to solve the Abdul dilemma. I tripped over a shovel but recovered without falling. The pain in my ankle was overshadowed by the fear of falling victim to the town matchmaker. "Oh, I'm not worried about being set up. I'm not even sure how long I will stay. I don't see enough to do here, and the quiet might be a little too much for me."

Pulling ahead of Bryce, I rounded the corner of the barn and found two large, black trash bags.

Bryce stood beside me. "You'd think the Andersons would have finished taking their trash to the dump. These are probably what is attracting your creature. You're lucky you haven't seen a black bear yet. They are very opportunistic and love to dig in people's trash." He began opening one of the bags.

I could sense the familiar, foul, decaying odor, the hairs on my arms and neck stood up. I knew the smell of a decomposing body very well.

Bryce dropped the bag and stepped back, covering his face with his shirt. "What the...?"

I couldn't help but quip, "Well, this is one way to solve the trash problem. Just wait for it to decompose."

Bryce gave me a disgusted look and I knew it was time for us to call the sheriff before I got myself into more hot water with the director.

So much for a low profile.

4

"*H*and over the bag, darlin'," I said calmly. I peeked inside the black plastic bag and immediately recognized the lower leg, thigh, and foot of a male. I closed it quickly for my new friend's sake, since his face turned as pale as a ghost and his breathing quickened like a racehorse. I placed it back in the same spot so as not to mess with the crime scene. "I think now would be a great time to introduce me to your dad."

Bryce pulled out his cell phone. "I'll send him a text. That way, he'll get the info faster even if he's busy charming the ladies. He always says it's not as rude to glance at your phone to read a message as it is to answer a call when someone is talking. Especially when it's me calling."

With Bryce trailing behind, I headed to the back deck and sat in a chair, waiting for Bryce's dad to arrive. We sat in silence, like a couple of statues.

Bryce leaned back in his chair and stared off into the distance, shaking his head gently.

With a sigh, I wondered how much trouble I'd be in with

the director for getting involved in a crime investigation before even unpacking my bags.

Sheriff Riddle arrived twenty minutes later, looking sharp in his tight-fitting, pressed uniform and shiny cowboy boots. He was definitely Bryce's dad, with his similar brown, curly hair and broad shoulders. He looked back and forth between Bryce and me.

"What took you so long, Dad?"

"I was at your Grandma Helen's house, listening to her talk about the town gossip. You know she doesn't like to be interrupted. I didn't see the text right away. Why are you at the old Anderson house, and who is this?" He reached out his open palm.

Bryce stood from his chair. "This is Ally Justice. She just moved in here, and I found her by the old barn."

Sheriff Riddle shook my hand. "Pleasure to meet you, Ally. I'm Joe Riddle. Welcome to the valley."

"Nice to meet you too, Sheriff. Sorry we had to meet under these circumstances."

He turned to Bryce. "You look pale. I'm assuming you didn't text me about an emergency just to meet our new neighbor. Why do you look like you just saw a ghost?"

Bryce stepped towards his dad. "We found some large, black trash bags. You need to look inside."

Sheriff Riddle shrugged. "It's not surprising the Andersons left stuff behind. They seemed to be in a hurry to move out. We can load them up in the pickup later and take them to the landfill."

"Dad, the trash bags are not the problem. It's what's inside. Let's go, now!" Bryce rushed towards the barn and motioned for his dad to follow.

Rounding the corner, Sheriff Riddle glanced back and forth between Bryce and me. He opened one of the bags to look inside and faced me. "How long ago did you arrive in our area?"

I recognized his tone, and for some reason, coming from the small-town sheriff, his narrowed gaze made my hackles rise. "I just got here yesterday afternoon. I haven't even come back this far on the property until now. If you're thinking I brought these, you can ask the taxi driver about my luggage. I think he would have noticed if I loaded stinking trash bags in his cab. Plus, these have been sitting here for over a week, judging by the ground underneath them. Also, these limbs have been detached from the victim for about a month, according to the stage of decay." I could hear the defensiveness in my voice and had no doubt he heard it too. "But don't worry, Sheriff Riddle, I'm not a suspect. I'm just the new girl in town who stumbled upon a crime scene straight out of a thriller novel. I'll be sure to bring my sleuthing skills to the table and help you crack this case." I said with a grin trying to lighten the mood.

Sheriff Riddle put his hands on his hips. "How do you know the length of time needed for a corpse to decay?"

I paused, inwardly chastising myself for acting like a forensic agent. "I work as a physical therapist. We learned a lot of details about the body in graduate school."

Sheriff Riddle tilted his head. "Including the stages of decay? I would assume you wouldn't last very long in your field if the people who you helped got to the point of decaying during your treatment."

"True, but the knowledge does help to describe and define how a person changes as we get older. I guess the professors figured they would be very thorough." If I planned to maintain my cover, I needed to be more careful in the future with spewing information about a crime scene.

Sheriff Riddle pulled out his phone. "I need to call the coroner to assist me with the scene.

A man arrived at the house in less than twenty minutes.

Seeing Dr. Dalton for the first time, I could quickly see the reason why Grandma Helen would consider it her personal mission to make some woman's life happier by marrying him. Ky Dalton stood over six feet tall, had light brown, slightly wavy hair, a chiseled jawline, and deep blue eyes. The subtle, woodsy scent of his cologne provided a welcome contrast to the smell of the decaying body. I rarely had time to even look at men in my line of work, but this guy's handsome, slightly rugged looks made him hard to ignore. He strutted across the terrain with a sense of confidence, letting me know he definitely doesn't spend all of his time inside an office.

The sheriff walked over and shook his hand.

"Dr. Dalton. Thanks for coming so quickly. This is Ally Justice." He pointed with an open hand. "We have a situation. Come with me."

Dr. Dalton stepped within inches of my toes and reached out to grab my hand. "Nice to meet you, Ally."

Embarrassed by his forward move, I stepped back. Reacting would have been easier if he posed a threat, but my body didn't see him as one, and my mind couldn't keep up. My legs weakened, and I noticed tingling in interesting places.

Sheriff Riddle led him around the back of the barn and stood back.

I followed with Bryce close behind. "Do you mind if I ask why the coroner would need to be present? The victim is obviously dead. Wouldn't assessment of the body be easier to complete at your office?"

Dr. Dalton opened one of the bags. "The answer to your question is, I prefer to see the body in the original location. The information helps with my part of the investigation. I am also the one responsible for removing evidence from the scene of the crime."

Dr. Dalton took photos of the bags in their original location and of the surrounding area.

Sheriff Riddle roped the area off with yellow crime scene tape.

The two worked harmoniously, making it obvious they had worked together for quite some time.

Afterwards, the doctor reached into his pocket and pulled out a bottle cap. He set it on the ground next to where the bags were found. He looked up at me and with a smirk "It's a bottle cap from a *Better Off Dead Pale Ale*, which is a local Colorado brew. I place one at each crime scene as a way of letting the deceased know I'm toasting their departure from this world, and also as a way to remind myself that the killer is still out there, better off dead."

I had no idea how to respond to his comment. "Well, it was nice to meet you. I'm going to the house. Let me know if you need anything else." I hurriedly scurried around the side of the barn, feeling like I was in an old-time movie where the killer was hot on my heels.

Hours later, after performing their investigation, I saw Dr. Dalton and the sheriff take the bags and leave, probably off to solve the case over a pint of "Better off Dead Pale Ale" at the local pub.

Bryce knocked on my door.

"You're still here," I exclaimed, as if he had just come back from the dead. I opened the door and stepped onto the porch.

Bryce smiled. "I thought I would say goodbye. Wow, what a way to welcome a new person to the town. Sorry you had to meet my dad and the doc under these circumstances. They are both really nice people. It's sometimes hard to tell, since they both work with criminals and dead people so much."

"Well, I will certainly have an interesting story to tell my friends back home," I said. I knew Director Sanchez would be less than excited, since I involved myself in an investigation after being in town less than forty-eight hours. He wouldn't call my actions laying low. Maybe I could blame the whole thing on Roos, since she chose this location.

"I guess I better go and start my chores before my dad gets home from work." He walked in the direction of his house and turned. "By the way, the animal was probably Barley."

I looked at him with my brows furrowed and my head tilted.

"He's been living in this barn for a few years. The Andersons let him come into their house at night to sleep and eat. He can be ornery at times, but he's a pretty cool cat overall. See ya later."

I watched him walk back towards his house, thinking Bryce would be a good connection to have since he knew so much about the town and its people.

Going back into the house to make dinner, I decided I would put a screen on the window, just as soon as I could go to the hardware store. I went to bed thinking having a sheriff as a neighbor could be a good or a bad thing. I was sure I would know before long how I really felt. One thing seemed clear; I would need to take some time after work tomorrow to walk around the property a little more. I didn't want any other surprises to draw attention in my direction.

Two hours passed before I drifted off to sleep. *Did Sheriff Riddle consider me a suspect even though I just arrived in the area? Would a small-town sheriff give credence to the forensic analysis I offered accidentally? Worse, would he be suspicious of me? Or would he actually believe the baloney I'd fed him about my education?* Only time would tell, and I made a mental note to stock up on alibis.

And alibis for my alibis.

Just in case.

5

I bolted upright in bed, my pajamas hugging to me like a clingy ex after a wild dream. I threw off the covers with a flourish, my eyes scanning the room for any clues as to where I was. Oh right, my new temporary bedroom. I was sure it would be temporary, just like my last three relationships.

We wish you a merry Christmas...

We wish you a merry Christmas...

The cube-shaped clock on the bedside table let out a loud screech, blaring a familiar song. I jumped, my heart racing. *How did that get turned on?* I must have hit a button last night while I was trying to figure out if the clock was even a clock or just a weird looking decoration. On one side, a mama bear wearing a Christmas hat clung to a tree, while on the other side, two cubs peered up at their mom. I searched for the off button as a low growling sound ended the song. I was pretty sure the clock was growling at me.

I dragged myself out of bed, knowing my first therapy appointment with Rita Garcia was in two hours. I had to be on time, or she'd give me a stern talking to. I knew from her file that she was the daughter of a Marine and grew up with strict schedules. I had no desire to be on the receiving end of any drill sergeant attitude.

The shower was a disaster, taking a solid five minutes to change from ice cold to scalding hot, and I wasted five more minutes finding a comfortable temperature. I raced through my shower and opened my suitcase, which Roos had packed for me. I dressed in khakis, a teal polo shirt, and a brand-new pair of shoes, the classic outfit of a physical therapist, but with a twist. The shoes Roos chose had a red, teal, and light blue mountain scene displayed on the sides. Several more shirts lay folded in the bag, each one matching the colors in the design of the shoes. I knew Roos must have had a good laugh while thinking of making me look so ridiculous... again. She would definitely hear an earful the next time I spoke with her.

I jogged downstairs and my mood brightened as the smell of freshly brewed coffee blasted me from the kitchen's automatic coffeemaker. I grabbed a breakfast bar, my cup of coffee, and my equipment bag, then ran out the door.

After a ten-minute drive, I arrived at Rita's house far too early. I rolled down my window and listened as the birds chattered in the trees, and my mind wandered to the body bags I'd found yesterday. Who would be stupid enough to stash the bags behind a barn right next door to the county sheriff? Only a local would know the house was vacant. The timing, too, would be difficult, given a sheriff didn't work an eight-to-five job in an office. He might come and go from his home throughout the day. Maybe the killer hoped the bags would be found by the bears and the body parts eaten.

Gross. But if that was the goal, why put them in plastic? Why not drop them in the woods and make finding dinner easier for the bears?

The idea of giant beasts feasting on a corpse just outside

the back door of my rental cabin shook me out of my thoughts. I scanned the trees around Rita's house, the hairs on my arms standing erect. The sound of the birds chirping in the forest suddenly stopped, and the eerie silence sent me rushing toward Rita's house. Maybe I was just imagining things, or maybe the killer was watching me right now. I can handle being stalked by killers easier than unknown wild animals.

Rita opened the door with a raised eyebrow as she glanced at her watch. "You look like you sprinted here. Your face is as red as a freshly smacked bottom."

I laughed. "You must be Rita. I am Ally Justice, your new physical therapist. It's nice to meet you."

"Likewise. I hope you can handle a feisty old lady. I don't want to see you cry," she said with a twinkle in her eye.

"Oh, I can handle just about anything. Speaking of which, where is your cane? I know you didn't get to where you are by teleportation," I quipped.

Rita took a long sip of her coffee and sighed. "I told the last gal I didn't need the cane anymore. I haven't run into a wall or fallen down the steps for at least a week."

The fifty-two-year-old woman, in surprisingly fit physical condition, invited me in. She took a seat in front of her bay window with a watchful eye as I stood holding my therapy bag. Her house sat at the top of Luker Mountain and had so many windows I could see most of the Lower Fork Valley, which made for a striking scene. The colors displayed an amazing combination of orange, green, and red. Speckled between the aspen trees stood evergreens and a vast array of wildflowers, which added the last touch to an amazing diversity of colors. The hodgepodge of vegetable pots and hanging flowers on the balcony of my apartment in D.C. paled in comparison to the stunning view.

Rita suffered a stroke two months ago, which caused her

depth perception to be impaired. Walking without a cane didn't help her negotiate her house safely. The prior therapist wrote a description of how she saved Rita from plunging head-first down the two steps leading into her garage.

Walking farther into the room, I checked the home for exits, and scanned what I could see through the open doors in the hallway, making note of a large gun safe in one of the bedrooms. Satisfied, I returned my attention to Rita. "Ok. I'll make you a deal. First, you tell me what the amazing smell is in your house. Second, you use your cane for one more week and, if you pass the balance test, I'll let you walk in the house without the annoying thing, and I won't nag you. The last thing you need is a broken hip on top of everything else."

Rita took a deep breath and exhaled loudly. "The smell is my famous green chili. I made this batch spicy enough you need a towel to wipe the sweat off your brow. As far as the cane, do they require you to be an overly paranoid person before you can become a physical therapist? Every therapist I have ever worked with has been uptight. I can't imagine any of you being very fun on a date. Maybe if you eat my chili, you will relax. I know it will loosen things up downtown." She laughed at her own joke, leaned back and grabbed her belly.

Turning to face her, I crossed my arms. "On the contrary. We have plenty of fun. Part of the fun includes torturing people like you, and getting paid for it. Now, grab your cane, and let's head outside to practice walking around your yard." I knew she would use the cane in front of me to appease me and ditch the thing the minute I left. This level of stubbornness must be exactly what helped women survive in rugged mountain towns. But that's okay. Everyone's got their quirks, and that's what makes it all the more interesting. Plus, if I'm lucky, I might just get to sample some of that famous green chili. Now that's something to look forward to!

Rita ambled across the room, grabbed the cane, and turned to face me. "All right, we have a deal. Can we start in the back of the property? I have the perfect activity for us." She reached down with her other hand and retrieved a black bag from the floor.

"Well, it depends on what you had in mind." The back door creaked as I pulled on the doorknob. I followed Rita, pausing to admire the hunting rifle propped up next to the door. "That thing loaded?"

"Wouldn't do much good, otherwise. I should probably tell you I won my fair share of shooting competitions when I was a teenager."

I nodded slowly. "Okay. Sounds interesting. Now I'm nervous about what you will want to do next."

She smiled with a slight tilt of her head. "I figure a great way for you to help me work on my balance and judgment skills is a little target practice."

I controlled the look of surprise and wrapped a gait belt around her waist. I pulled on the cool, jagged front clasp to test the belt's tautness. "Where do you suggest we do such an activity?"

Already headed out the back door, she lifted the cane and pointed toward a path which led from the back of her property.

I hesitantly followed her. "Is this all your property?"

"Technically speaking, yes, it is, since I pay taxes. The government designated the land as Bureau of Land Management, or BLM for short. I figure I can use the space just as much as anyone else."

"Are you sure the BLM condones awkward, clumsy ladies shooting guns on their property?"

"First of all, I am working with you to fix the clumsiness, and second of all, I used to be state champ. My dad taught me how to shoot a gun at the age of five, and I practiced every chance I got. I can shoot the acorn out of a running squirrel's mouth." She stuck out her chest and chin.

Stubborn. I liked her. "All right, but if you fall over from the recoil, I'm moving on to my next patient." I followed her down the path surrounded by oak brush, aspen trees, and cactus to an opening with various orange-colored targets about fifty yards away. The smell of sage and pine, combined with the beautiful scenery, relaxed me slightly.

Then, she reached into the bag and pulled out a Glock 22 9mm pistol.

She achieved a stance she must have used when she was younger. Not having the balance, she once had, she stumbled. I reached for the belt attached to her waist and pulled hard on the strap until the cloth tightened in my palm.

"Stop stressing, Ally. I am just getting back into my groove."

Letting go of the belt, I covered my ears with my hands.

She widened her stance, brought the gun in front of her with a slight bend in both elbows, and began pulling the trigger. She emptied a full clip at the targets, hitting them eleven out of fifteen times.

My arms dropped to my side. "Seventy-five percent efficiency! I didn't expect you to do so well."

"My record will improve if we can work on this together a few more times. Then, I will know I am back in the game and recovering from this stupid stroke."

What she said sounded like a good plan to her but not me. I chalked this experience up to the most dangerous therapy session I ever participated in. I mean, who knew that physical therapy could be such a trigger-happy experience?

After walking her back to her house, I said my goodbyes and reminded her of next week's appointment.

After I loaded my gear in the SUV, I texted Roos to inquire whether she had intel on Fahid's current location. Abdul would, undoubtedly, have him looking for me and I would be ready.

y next patient, Helen, lived thirty minutes away in the boondocks. I drove along the winding, two-lane road, watching for deer. The cashier at the grocery store warned me about the animals, which were known to graze on the random tufts of grass poking through the cracked asphalt. But these deer were different, they were like the mafia of the forest, standing still along the side of the road and staring at me as if they were saying *You better watch it, buddy.*

Almost to her house, I noticed a group of three does standing still along the side of the road. I slowed, expecting them to run. Instead, they paused, watching me approach. The fact they didn't move gave me the impression they had no concern about a large, moving vehicle interrupting their meal. One of them nonchalantly walked across the road within a few feet of the front of my car. The other two sauntered behind her, looking straight at me as if saying, *Didn't you see the deer crossing sign, you idiot?*

According to the previous therapist, my next patient Helen Riddle, a 61-year-old woman, lived an interesting life as the mother of the local sheriff. Her interactions with her son provided entertainment for those lucky enough to be in the same room.

On more than one occasion, the sheriff burst into Helen's house during a therapy session to reprimand her for being involved in police business.

Helen, apparently, heard a lot of juicy information in the local Bingo Hall and would tell her son she had a duty to help protect her neighbors.

From what, exactly, no one knew.

Helen's residence, a two-story log house with a deck which wrapped around half of the upstairs, was typical of the homes in the area. Her gravel driveway wound back and forth in a steep and narrow line. Multiple types of green shrubs and groundcover lined the sides of the driveway, some displaying stunning white and purple flowers. They filled the air with a soft, sweet aroma. At the top sat a recessed area which allowed just enough room for a vehicle to turn around. Most of the scenery surrounding her home grew naturally, but she did have a small, green lawn which wrapped around to the back of the house.

I walked up the paved path with my tool bag dragging behind me, the sound of gravel crunching under my decorative new shoes. Once at the door, I rang the doorbell.

"Enter," yelled a voice from inside.

Opening the door slowly and stepping inside, I saw Helen sitting in the front room. She had long, straight silver hair and dressed in a blue button up floral shirt with solid teal pants.

She stared at a large computer monitor with a cup of steaming liquid in her hand. "Come on in, Ally. I'll be done in a minute. I'm typing a message to a young woman on a dating site."

"Looking for a dinner date?" I teased.

Helen scooted forward in her seat. "Not for myself. I gave up dating a while ago, when the sheriff's dad passed. I'm finding a wife for my son."

"Don't you think he can take care of that himself?"

"Nope. He stalled for too long so I handled the task myself. If I wait for him, I'll never have more grandbabies. I could die tomorrow."

I grinned. The sheriff clearly had his hands full. "You ready?"

Helen gulped what was left in her mug. "I needed a cup of coffee to help give me the energy to handle what you will put me through. I know what P. T. stands for: pain and torture. But I'm ready for it, bring on the pain and torture, I'm ready to take on whatever you throw at me! After all, I have the strength of a thousand deer and the wisdom of a bingo hall hoodlum."

Rolling my eyes, I shook my head. "You're not the first person to perpetuate the same rumor. We therapists get a bad rap for no good reason. How's the hip feeling?"

Helen laughed. "Well, considering I use to ski sixty days in a season, and the last few years I hit the slopes only six times because of the pain in my hip, I feel pretty good. At first, I didn't know if having a hip replacement was a smart idea. Now, I realize I waited too long. I missed some sweet powder days for nothing."

"The irony of you accusing me of a plan to torture you when you already inflicted the pain on yourself is amusing." I chuckled. "No, seriously, you aren't alone. A lot of my patients say the same thing about waiting. The surgery is pretty aggressive. Have you ever watched the procedure on You Tube?"

Helen placed her hands on her hips, her eyes wide-open. "Are you crazy? If I did, I would have never even thought about having the operation. Let the folks who make the big bucks deal with all of the gruesome stuff. I just want to walk without pain so I can beat the women who take up three tables at Bingo with all of their crap. The game is hard enough with old, drunk Frank slurring the numbers. I sit up front, or I can't understand him, and I miss stamping my card."

"Isn't there a board listing the digits they call out?" A beeping sound came from the back of the house.

Helen glanced in the direction of the noise. "Sure. But he forgets to put some of them up there, so if you didn't understand him the first time he said it, then you are screwed! Sometimes, my grandson, Bryce, goes with me. He has better hearing. I win more dough when he attends. Plus, our situation is a win/win. I buy him soda and snacks, and he feeds me the rumors he hears at school. His gossip is even better than the four-one-one the church ladies give out. He's like my own personal bingo spy."

I laughed. "Four-one-one? Where did you hear that one?"

"I told you. Bryce teaches me lots of things." Helen clapped once. "Oh! I forgot to offer you a cup of coffee. You want some? The stuff will tear the lining out of your esophagus."

"Sounds amazing but no, thanks. One revved-up engine in this therapy session is enough. Let's get started. Grab your walker, and we'll head into the living room." I retrieved my tool bag and carried it to the living room where she still had the exercise band around a table leg. A large, gray sectional couch filled the area and surrounded a marble coffee table. A rectangular, mahogany table took up most of the adjacent dining room. A white, semi-ornamental brick fireplace covered the far wall, with a stamped metal cowboy riding a bucking horse hanging above the mantel made of a log.

Across the room hung a clock with various birds depicting the hour.

"Let's do the band exercises your therapist taught you last time. I usually know if my patients did not do their homework when they end up tangled in the band," I joked. "Give me twelve reps each direction. Hold on to the back of the chair for balance."

Helen let out a heavy sigh. "Boy, are you a ball buster! Just about as bad as old Chester Riley. When I did some book work for his plumbing business, he hassled me daily about getting people to pay their bills. Like I had any control over whether the deadbeat customers paid or not."

"Don't worry, Helen, I'm probably not as bad as old Chester. But I do want to make sure you can walk without pain and beat those women at bingo. And who knows, maybe with all that extra energy, you'll be able to find a way to make those deadbeat customers pay up too." I grinned. "Now let's get to work, we've got bingo to win."

Helen stepped into the band and began the exercise. "Bryce told me he saw a mound of fresh dirt in the back of Chester Riley's property several weeks ago. He suspects a body might have been buried there. And yesterday, Joey found some black trash bags on the old Anderson property with chopped-up body parts. Maybe Chester found a new way to collect his money."

"Wow! That's how gossip gets started." I laughed. "Face the chair and pull the band forward." My mind registered the potential intel, and I promised myself I would consider the information later.

Helen pointed a finger. "You want real gossip; you should hang out with the church ladies. They're like the CIA of small towns. Besides, you are brand new to the area. Who are you going to tell?"

I didn't bother to inform her I found the bags on the

property. I shrugged. "I guess no one. Did they figure out who the body belongs to?"

"I asked Joey. He said they just started their investigation. I bet the body parts belong to one of the homeless people who live in the mountains. Something is always happening to them."

My mind reeled, keeping up with Helen's rapid change of topics. "Homeless people? In the mountains? I thought they only lived in the city. Where do they stay?"

Helen turned to kick her leg out to the side. "They have a few places. The railroad goes right next to the Colorado River on the south side. Some of the homeless expanded a few naturally created caves for a small living space. The locals call them the Hobo Hotels. Some also stay up on the hogbacks."

I bent down to help her switch the band to the other leg, my knees popping and cracking loudly. "What are hogbacks?"

Helen laughed. "I guess I am not the only one with bad joints. The hogbacks are what we call the mountains spread throughout the area. They resemble a hog's back. I'm not sure who came up with the term."

"Wouldn't a mountain be a dangerous place to live with so many animals who could eat them?" I instantly pictured a person being dragged out of a cave by a giant, brown bear. "What about bears?"

Helen shook her head. "Actually, it's the mountain lions you have to worry about."

My heart rate increased. I swallowed. "Mountain lions?"

Helen patted my shoulder. "Don't worry about it, honey. We haven't had a mountain lion attack for at least a week. The homeless people know how to survive. They create shelter under the root system of the twisted pine trees. The dead trees create a cave-like area with their intertwined branch system."

"So, do the residents of the town want them to leave?"

Helen turned her body to perform the next exercise. "No. Some of them are people who moved to the area to ski. They don't want to hold a job so they live in the mountains and pick up manual labor here and there when they need money to buy a lift ticket. No harm done." She finished the last of the series of exercises. "I never did fully understand the idea of living out in the open just to have time to play. Joey would never let me live in such conditions, anyway."

"I don't think I could live in a place out in the open for long. I wouldn't get enough sleep. Let's do a lap down to the mailbox and back using your walker."

Helen chuckled. "Well, I guess we all have our different priorities. Mine is to beat those bingo ladies and yours is to not be dragged away by a mountain lion. Let's get moving."

Helen and I walked down the paved path and onto the gravel driveway leading to her mailbox. She had a bright red, rolling walker with large wheels on the front and a black seat with a storage compartment underneath. The gravel protested under the weight of the walker. The steep driveway caused her to pick up speed so Helen held on to the brakes the entire way down to the mailbox. Her mailbox was decorated with an old pair of skis and a ski boot, which seemed appropriate for the area.

She opened the door, grabbed her mail, and placed the stack in the compartment under the seat. "How about I sit down on the walker and you push me back up the hill?" she suggested. She breathed heavily.

My eyes scanned the driveway, and I searched the trees for movement. "I would, but then my reputation as a ball-buster would be ruined. Therapy patients throughout the valley will think I'm soft. They'll force me to sit with them and sip on hot cocoa instead of making them work."

Helen pushed the brake levers to the lock position. "I wouldn't want you to drink hot cocoa on a daily basis. But I can keep a secret. No one will know if you show me mercy. I'll tell everyone you were never here."

Cocking my head to the side, I smirked. "How did I get the information about the black trash bags with body parts and the mound of dirt at Chester Riley's house?"

She huffed, yanked the brakes off and started up the hill. The walker tipped sideways.

I reached for the soft foam covering at the front of the walker and widened my stance to balance the load. With my other hand, I grabbed her gait belt and pulled backwards, feeling the strain of her body weight in my neck and shoulders.

Helen took two small steps to recover. "You're my therapist. Information we share has to be kept confidential."

Walking beside her, I kept one hand on the walker. "I'm a physical therapist, not a private investigator. Although, I do have my own theories about what might be buried on Chester Riley's property. But let's focus on getting you up the hill."

Moving slowly, I guided us to the top of the driveway and into the house with three rest breaks. Looking around, I took the opportunity to point out her many bird feeders, flower beds, and the giant pickup in her driveway, with two steps up into the cab. "That your truck?"

"Joey got that for me last winter. He took the keys, but he promised to drive me to Bingo."

My mind registered that the truck had a running board. I doubted Helen could climb into the cab in her current condition.

Back inside, she plopped down in a chair at the table, the old wood creaking from the sudden load.

Leaning over her, I removed the gait belt. "Our next appointment is on Friday at eleven o' clock. Does the time still work for you?"

"I'll be waiting. This time, I'll drink a whole pot of coffee. You just about killed me."

As I packed up my bag and said my goodbyes, I couldn't help but chuckle to myself. Helen may have been a bit of a gossip, but she was also a tough cookie and a great patient. I couldn't wait to see what kind of wild rumors and insights she would share with me during our next session.

7
_____

*M*y workday ended with me seeing two more patients and feeling like I needed a drink. Afterwards, I drove back home and changed into leggings, a sports bra, and a shirt that said *Be nice or shut up* because let's face it, some people just need a reminder. My orders were to lay low and be a wallflower, but being swept away from exciting missions got boring fast. I thought to myself, "would participating in a little investigative work hurt? I don't think so." I grabbed my trusty nine-millimeter and went for a hike on the hogback to find the homeless shelters Helen mentioned. My chest tightened almost immediately as I struggled to pace my breathing, the path ascending rapidly. I felt like I was trying to breathe through a straw, and it made me dizzy and light-headed. I stopped frequently to catch my breath and take in the view.

The trail wound back and forth across the mountain like a drunk snake. After traveling for a short time, I took a sip from my bottle, thankful for the cool, sweet taste of the recovery drink. I arrived at the point where the trees parted, showing a sky view of the town. The Colorado River meandered through the valley next to the highway. In the distance, the sun set in the west. The sky was a beautiful array of oranges and reds, and I paused, listening to the sound of my heartbeat in my ears and throat. I scanned back and forth across the mountain, watching for bears or mountain lions. I thought to myself, "Why would they live in a place so close to humans? Do they enjoy the sound of car horns and sirens?"

As the trail took two one-hundred-and-eighty-degree turns and straightened out, I spotted a dead tree whose twisted roots created a cave. They tangled and turned but still left enough room for one person to crawl underneath. I bent forward to look inside and spotted a ragged blanket, faded backpack, and discarded water bottles. I grabbed my nine-millimeter and got down on my knees to have a closer look. Given the amount of dirt on and around the items, I guessed no one had touched them for several weeks. I wondered if the person who lived here was a slob or just really into the "rugged mountain man" look.

Leaning back on my knees, I pulled my business phone out of my pack and took a few pictures of the scene for later use. I had no idea whether all of the homeless residences looked the same as this one. Did the person who lived here have anything to do with the body parts? I intended to find out.

As I trekked back to the house, a shrill ringing noise came from the burner phone. I knew the caller could only be someone from work. "Hello."

"Evans, it's Cunningham. How are things going there?"

His words sounded rushed. "I wondered how much time would pass before you called." I tried to keep the tone of desperation out of my voice. "Ah, it's going fine."

Cunningham paused before responding. "You don't sound convincing. What's happening?"

"Well, I spent the day seeing patients. I've met the sheriff, town doctor, coroner, and the sheriff's son. I'd say I am keeping busy."

"The sheriff and the coroner? What kind of trouble are you getting into? You are supposed to keep your head down. Be invisible," he warned.

"The sheriff's son came over to visit. The house you rented for me is next door. When we were looking for a skunk, we found two black trash bags full of human body parts." I cringed, the butterflies swarming in my stomach, and waited for the yelling to begin. I liked Cunningham, despite his habit of harassing me. Being yelled at resembled taking a dressing-down from my father. Not fun.

"First of all, why would you be looking for a skunk? Second of all, you have been there less than seventy-two hours, and you already dug up some body parts?" he questioned.

I couldn't help but chuckle to myself, "Well, when life gives you lemons... or in this case, when life gives you a skunk problem, find some body parts instead. And as for the timing, I guess I just have a knack for finding trouble" I replied with a hint of sarcasm.

The familiar feeling of being a disappointment weighed down my shoulders like a wet blanket. "The skunk turned out to be my new pet cat, Barley. I had nothing to do with the body parts, other than I found them on the rental property."

"So, you have already become a suspect in a homicide. Didn't I ask you to lay low? I told you to avoid drawing attention to yourself!"

The volume of his voice grew with each word. My grip on the phone tightened. "Again, sir, I didn't put the body parts there. I told Sheriff Riddle the timeline had to be wrong for any possible involvement on my part. Maybe he understood. I'm not sure how smart these small-town sheriffs are. An individual gave me intel saying the victim might be one of their homeless people in the area. I hiked up something called a hogback this evening to take a look, and I'm just heading back home now."

"Who provided the intel? You talked to others about the case?"

I heard the director's stern voice in the background.

"Director Sanchez wants me to remind you that if you are arrested, your prints will pop up, and that town will be swarming with Abdul's people in a matter of hours."

"It's not like that. I'm fine. One of my patients is the sheriff's mother, and the grandmother of the boy who was with me when I found the bags. She knows a lot of things about the area. I didn't even tell her I found the bags, or I knew about the body."

"All right. Stay out of the investigation. We haven't had eyes on Abdul's brother for two days. The director is concerned he might have found out about your relocation. Be inconspicuous."

My pulse quickened followed by the calm feeling I achieved before my missions. "Roger that, sir."

"I mean underground, low."

"Got it. Did the director give you any idea about how long I have to stay here?" I could practically smell the stench of the director's conversation-ending cigar through the phone.

"I don't think anything will change right now with the way things are heating up here. I'll be in touch." He hung up.

The information stirred in my brain like a pot of soup. He didn't need to know about my plan to find out the identity of the victim and who murdered him. I would be discreet and professional. Besides, Sheriff Riddle needed all the help he could muster. I thought to myself, "Maybe I'll even give him some pointers on how to properly catch a skunk, or maybe not."

8

When I returned to my cozy little cabin, I was greeted by none other than Barley the black cat, lounging on the front porch like he owned the place (which, let's be real, he probably did). Just as I was about to give him a friendly pat on the head, I noticed a lump behind him. My hand instinctively reached for my trusty nine (you know, just in case it was a mountain lion in disguise). But before I could even pull it out, the lump moved and I saw it was just an Australian Shepherd, taking a nap in the sun.

"I see you've met Beano," said a smooth voice from behind me. I turned to see none other than Dr. Superman himself (ok, fine, his name is Ky Dalton) standing there looking like he just walked off a romance novel cover. I mean, honestly, what is it with small towns and their too-good-to-be-true residents?

"What kind of name is Beano?" I asked, trying to shake off the distraction of his chiseled jawline. Beano's tail thumped loudly against the porch floor.

Dr. Dalton chuckled. "Well, you see, Beano belongs to Frank Livingston who lives just up the river. Frank is often at the Bingo Hall and when he's had a drink or two, he slurs the name Bingo, so we just call him Beano. He's like the town dog, everyone loves him."

"I heard about Frank. Sounds like I need to check out this Bingo Hall," I said with a grin.

Dr. Dalton's smile could light up a room. "I'd be happy to take you. It's like a live performance, you have to see it at least once."

As if on cue, Beano let out a contented sigh and began to groom himself.

I couldn't help but notice the awkward silence that followed. "So, what brings you back to the house? I'm pretty sure we've found all the body parts by now." I gave him a dry look.

Hot Stuff cleared his throat. "I came to ask you a few questions," he said, looking a little sheepish.

"Shoot," I said, stroking Beano's soft fur.

"Sheriff Riddle said you arrived in the area two days ago. Is that correct?"

"Yes, I did. I already told Sheriff Riddle and gave him my travel information. I flew into DIA and then took a death-trap puddle jumper to the airport into a town called Shale. From there, I took a taxi to Shotgun. Why do you ask?"

Dr. Dalton stepped up on the porch and started petting Beano, who let out a happy groan and continued his nap. "Just getting some background. What brought you to Shotgun?"

I couldn't help but roll my eyes. "Sue Morrison hired me to work at Mountain Tops Home Health Agency as a P.T. I would think you would know since you own the place."

Ky looked up from Beano, a hint of amusement in his eyes. "Touché. I'll make sure to keep my questions more relevant in the future." Ky brushed his fingers through his hair. "I do own the place, but I keep my distance, since I am also the referring provider. I don't want any misunderstandings about who gets home health and who doesn't. Most of the decisions are dictated by the insurance company, anyway. Mountain Tops is really run by Sue, my manager."

He paused and I couldn't help but think "Yeah, and I bet she's a real ball-buster."

Stepping over to where Barley laid, I stroked his satin fur. "She seems to be doing a pretty good job keeping the place organized. Why would you be out here doing the investigation? Isn't that Sheriff Riddle's job?"

Ky let out a chuckle. "Oh, I'm not investigating. I'm just asking questions. It's a small town, which means we share duties. Every new bit of information helps me to figure out what might have happened to the murder victim. You were the first one to see the remains. Or, I guess, maybe the second." He pulled up his pants and jutted out his chin.

"What happened to the body is that a deranged murderer killed him and chopped his body up," I said. "You don't need high-level forensic skills to determine the kind of person who would commit such a crime. Now, if you don't mind, I need to start some dinner." I turned abruptly and stepped towards the entrance.

"Does this mean a trip to the Bingo Hall is off the table?" Ky asked.

I took a deep breath, aware of my firm grip on the door handle. "I'm pretty busy with my new job. Maybe in a few weeks, after I've settled in?" By then, I'd be out of this one-horse town.

Dr. Dalton took the hint and left.

No wonder such a good-looking man was still single. I patted my leg to signal Beano to follow me inside. Beano's presence gave me a sense of security which I normally got from my weapons. If my home served as one of his many residences, I'd easily acclimate to having him around. I paced the house, still irritated from my conversation with Dr. Dalton.

Beano watched me for a few minutes and then jumped up on the couch and laid down.

Grabbing my keys off of the hook, I made the decision to leave my new friend alone on the couch sleeping. I didn't plan to be long. I went outside and jumped in the SUV in search of a gardening center.

When I was a child, gardening was my favorite hobby and something which relieved my stress. Not only was I good at growing plants, I succeeded without having a lot of space to use, since I always lived in the city. Even though I didn't plan on staying in the area long, digging in the dirt would help me relax.

The local hardware store was still open so I took my time picking out several tomato, cucumber, squash, and pepper plants, figuring I would start with the basics and expand my garden with time. I noticed a spot where the previous owners planted a garden, which meant the preparation would be minimal.

Once I got home, I let Beano out and worked until dark putting the plants into the ground with precision. I watered the new garden carefully and stood back to admire my work. The tension left my body and only excitement remained. After I cleaned my mess, I went inside to make a microwave dinner, wishing I already had fresh cucumbers and toma-toes from my new garden to make a salad, but knowing that in due time, I would have the freshest and tastiest ingredi-ents for all my meals. And maybe, just maybe, I'll invite Dr. Dalton over for dinner and show him that I'm not just a city slicker, but a green thumb too. *Ugh. Stay focused Ally.*

As I sat to eat and watch TV, the doorbell rang. I hoped my visitor was not Dr. Superman coming back to ask more questions. Checking to make sure I could easily reach my nine, I opened the door and found Rita, Helen, and Bryce standing there together. "Hi. What are you three doing here? I wasn't expecting a visit from the Three Musketeers."

Helen ran her fingers through her hair. "We were hanging out with Bryce while the sheriff was out fighting crime. We saw Dr. Dalton's car in the driveway. I've been trying to set him up with a worthy woman and you caught his attention after being in town for just a short time? I would say that is fine work."

"Why thank you, Helen, I didn't know you had such high standards for me," I said with a chuckle.

Helen pushed past me, nearly running over my foot with her walker, and made herself at home.

Rita, not using her cane of course and Bryce followed.

I walked into the living room, the show I watched still running. The host of the Guns and Ammo Show talked in a deep voice about a new suppressor. Eager to draw attention from the show, I stepped in front of the television. "I didn't know you knew each other."

"Rita and I go way back," Helen said. "She has known me since my husband died, and I struggled to raise Joey on my own. So, what did Dr. Handsome want?"

"Oh, you mean Dr. Superman?" I corrected. "He asked me questions about when I arrived and other details. I think he is working up possible suspects."

Rita placed her hands on her hips. "But you just came to town. Bryce was with you when you found the bags. There's no way he would consider you a suspect. Why are you calling him Dr. Superman?"

Moving over to the couch, I sat down and motioned for the others to follow. "Because he is obviously full of himself. What kind of person works as a doctor, coroner, and investigator? No wonder he is single. In no way could he have time for a woman, especially considering his cocky manner. A girlfriend would have a difficult time competing with his ego."

Helen smiled. "It's a small town. He does all of those things to keep from getting bored. He's actually a really nice man. He is just picky about who he lets in his life. Most of the local single girls are after him because he is a doctor. They want security, but his personality goes much deeper."

My fingers played with strands of my hair. "Yeah, maybe. I'm not looking for security, so I plan to stay away. I need to focus on my work."

Rita waved her hand. "Work is overrated. Do you think the victim is someone from around here?"

"I heard my dad on the phone with Dr. Dalton," Bryce said. He sat up straighter in his seat. "The DNA results will be back by tomorrow morning. I can let you know what they find."

I shook my head, trying to hide my amusement. "Bryce, I appreciate your eagerness to help, but I think it's best if we leave the detective work to the professionals. Besides, I don't want to be an accomplice to your cybercrime shenanigans."

Bryce glanced at Helen. "My dad works from a computer at home sometimes. I know his password. I've helped a couple of buddies at school get out of trouble."

Helen chimed in, "But don't worry, if you need any real detective work done, you can always count on the Three Musketeers. We'll solve this mystery in no time. And we probably won't even break any laws." We all shared a laugh, and I couldn't help but feel grateful for the new friends I had made in this small town.

My stomach growled as a reminder I didn't have a chance to finish my dinner. "I went for a hike today on the hogback to check out where one of the homeless men lives. It doesn't look like anyone has been there for about a month. The scenario matches the timeline. I figure, after work tomorrow, I will go to the Hobo Hotels and ask some questions." The thought occurred to me the director would not define my actions as laying low, but the idea of solving a crime made me miss my job and my home less. I couldn't help but crave the excitement.

"Be careful," Rita warned. "Sometimes they don't like having visitors. They are afraid they will get kicked out of their homes."

I shrugged. "Oh, I can handle myself. I am not too worried."

"Did they teach you about homeless people in P. T. school, too?" Bryce asked.

"My dad was a tough man. He taught me life skills, since I was an only child. I think he wanted a son but got me instead. I was just happy to have his attention, so I listened closely to whatever he said." I left out the details about the agency expanding on those skills until I became a highly trained and indispensable agent.

"We better let you finish your dinner," Rita said. "We'll be in touch tomorrow, once we have more information."

Standing up from the couch, I opened the door for the three of them to leave.

Rita, the first one to exit, tripped over the rug. She barely caught herself on the railing of the porch. She glanced back briefly and furled her brows, wiped her hands on her pants and kept walking without a word.

"Looks like our resident detective might have some competition," I joked. "Rita, watch out for that rug, it's a real trip-master!"

Rita's smooth moves are bound to draw attention to us at an inopportune time. Hopefully, not from the wrong people.

9

When I woke up in the morning, I took my cup of coffee and went outside to check on my new garden. But when I saw that only half of my plants remained, I gasped in shock. As I looked around frantically, I spotted the white butt of a deer strolling away from the scene of the crime, looking as if it had just won the lottery. Her slow, casual gait indicated she didn't see me as a threat, but I saw her smirk and knew she had done it on purpose. My mind raced as I searched for a way to retaliate against her blatant destruction of my property. I knew I had little time to dress for work, so I went back inside with one thought in my head, *This is war, and I don't plan to lose. I'll build a fence, that'll do it.*

After work, I changed clothes and stopped by the Hobo Hotels, a series of small caves in the side of the mountain, above the railroad tracks. From outside, I saw ragged blankets and threadbare cloth bags strewn across the floor. The only man there frowned when he saw me. He wore three hats, each stacked on top of the other, three layered coats and jackets, baggy blue pants, and tan work boots. Judging by the pungent smell in the air, he had not washed anything recently. I had to restrain myself to keep from asking why he wore the odd outfit.

"Who are you? And what do you want?" he demanded, stomping towards me with fists clenched.

"My name is Ally. I'm the new home health physical therapist in the area." I refrained from reaching out to shake his hand, since his hands were covered in dirt.

He turned his back and moved things around. "Well, I don't need physical therapy and, as you can see, this isn't much of a home."

"Oh. I'm not here to give you therapy. I was exploring yesterday and hiked on the hogback in the middle of town. I came across a small cave built under the roots of a tree. The space had a blanket and some other items and looked like it had been empty for a while. I wondered if you might know who lived there," I said, trying not to sound too nosy.

The man looked me up and down. "That was where Kevin Jankins hung out. He didn't like staying over here. He said the sound of the trains bothered him. We haven't seen him in several weeks. We all figured he moved on to greener pastures."

I looked around at the other small rooms. "Does anyone else know Kevin? Someone who might know where he went?"

"Well, considering he is the son of Mr. Hotshot district attorney, a lot of people know him." He removed his hats and scratched the top of his head. "The problem is, he and the family had a falling out. He hadn't spoken with them in over three years. He never did fit into that family. They were always outdoing each other, trying to be the most important person in town."

"Did Kevin usually take off for extended periods of time?" I asked, trying to sound casual.

"Not usually. When someone leaves their spot, another person is usually there to take over. Best to stick around if you want to keep your space. I did hear a mountain lion was spotted up there last week. Maybe people were just waiting until the big cat moved on," he said with a chuckle.

The thought sent chills down my spine. "A mountain lion? I hiked where a mountain lion lives?" I exclaimed.

He laughed. "They don't usually stay for long unless there's prey nearby. The hogback is surrounded by people and houses. Lions usually avoid people, unless the cat is sick or really, really hungry. Then, one might try to eat you." He chuckled again, but I couldn't help but feel a little uneasy.

The concept of being hunted by a mountain lion seemed ridiculous and unbelievable, but I couldn't shake the image of the beast ripping out my throat. Trying to maintain my cool, I breathed in deeply and slowly exhaled. "I hope not. I had no idea I was on the menu during my hike."

"Probably not. Mountain lion attacks on humans are rare," he said with a chuckle.

"Well, I guess I'll have to stick to gardening and leave the mountain lion hunting to the professionals," I said trying to make light of the situation. "I guess, if you live out in the open, you have to know a lot about the dangers around you. Well, thanks for the information. Sorry for interrupting your nap."

"That's all right. Not much to do around here until ski season, anyway," he said with a shrug.

"You go skiing?" I said, with a little too much surprise in my voice. He didn't look like the athletic type.

"Yeah. A lot of us do. We came to this area to ski. The problem is, living in the valley is so expensive, most of the people who live here end up working all of the time. They don't have time to ski. It's a total waste. We make a choice to live simply, pick up jobs which pay just enough money to buy food and lift tickets but don't take up all of our time," he explained.

"Sounds like a smart choice. Have a good one." I turned and walked back to the car. I could appreciate the diversity amongst the people who lived in the vicinity. I guess, when something like the majestic mountains exist, a wide variety of people find themselves living in one small area.

When I walked inside my front door, my business phone buzzed with a call from Rita, whose phone number I stored earlier when I confirmed our appointment.

"Hey! Get dressed. Helen, Bryce and I are going to play some Bingo, and you're coming with us."

She sounded more energetic than I felt. "Bingo? Bingo is not really my game." As soon as I rejected her idea, I realized the Bingo Hall might be a good place to pick up some information on the district attorney's family. "But I guess I do want to watch this Frank guy in action."

Rita whistled. "Wow! That took a lot less convincing than I thought. Pick you up in twenty minutes."

I bounded up the stairs to find an outfit to wear. Just what does someone wear to play Bingo? I decided on jeans, a t-shirt, and tennis shoes. I wanted to be comfortable and able to move quickly. I might need to keep Rita from running into tables and help lift Helen up out of a chair if she had trouble.

Rita drove us all to the Bingo Hall in a midnight blue sports car.

The inside smelled like a combination of leather and Armor All. I sat, with Bryce, in the back, which meant my knees landed just inches away from my chest. Breathing quickly became difficult. "I'm guessing this is probably not the ideal car to drive in the mountains when it is snowing. What happened to the four-wheel drive?"

Rita gripped the steering wheel. "This is my spring and

summer ride. In the winter, I drive a sensible vehicle, just like all of the other mountain women. I'm not about to sport a slow, grumbly SUV in the summer when I can lay the pedal of this beauty to the ground."

I couldn't help but roll my eyes at her midlife crisis-like behavior. "At my house, I watched you stumble while walking because you are still misjudging distances. I'm not sure I want to watch you make the same mistake going eighty miles an hour," I said, trying to sound concerned.

But Rita just pressed down on the gas pedal even harder. My neck couldn't hold my head in place, my ponytail rammed the headrest, and my stomach tickled my spine.

"The faster I go, the smoother I move. It's pure science. You should know that with all of your high-level schooling," Rita said with a grin, as if that explained everything.

I couldn't help as I grabbed the oh-crap handle above the door. "I'm a movement specialist, and I can say you are definitely lying. Tell me when we are there so I can open my eyes."

When we arrived at the Bingo Hall, I realized I had been holding my breath the whole way. A lot more cars were in the parking lot than I expected. Apparently, the sum total of entertainment in the valley was Bingo and going to the library.

I waited, with the others, in the bar downstairs, since the Bingo Hall wasn't open yet. Surprisingly, they allowed Bryce in the bar despite his not being of age. I walked towards a four-top table, my tennis shoes sticking to the floor with each step. "When do we go upstairs?"

"They don't open for a half an hour," Rita said. "We get here early so we can get a table up close. Being at the front makes it easier to understand Frank, if you can stand the smell of whiskey wafting off of his breath."

A bearded man turned around from his seat at the bar top. He must have heard his name. He waved.

Helen waved back with a toothy smile. "Since you move faster than us, we'll put you in front of the door with Bryce. Run to the front tables and save three. Lily will be right behind you, so don't let her intimidate you. Beat her to them and spread out."

I couldn't help but chuckle at their strategic Bingo plan. "So now I know why you really invited me. And who is Lily?" I looked around, taking notice of the other people in the bar for the first time. A baseball game played loudly on the TV over the bar, and glasses clinked together as the bartender prepared drinks for her customers.

"She's the wife of Don Jankins, the district attorney." Helen leaned forward. "She works as a realtor so she can set her own schedule. She schmoozes the townspeople so they let her have her way in the Bingo Hall. I think she has a secret gambling addiction."

I placed my elbows on the table, and smiled. "I think you might need to look in the mirror. You're the ones with the attack plan."

Bryce laughed.

I sat back and rubbed the sticky feeling on my elbows left behind by my momentary contact with the poorly washed table.

"The way the hall was built makes the sound travel forward," Helen said. "The front is the best place to hear what the others are talking about. Sitting there is how I find out about everything happening in town." She rubbed her hands together and looked around at the other patrons. "By the way, is that the future mother of my grandchildren I see?" she asked Rita. She pointed towards the bar.

Rita put her hand on her forehead. "Oh, no. Not again. You can't keep pressuring these poor new girls..."

Helen was already making her way over to the bar.

"Here we go." Rita covered her eyes with a hand for several seconds before lowering her palm to the table with a sigh. "Helen just can't help herself."

I watched with amusement as Helen leaned across the bar and waved the bartender over. She stood about five-foot-eight, with long, thick brown hair and a firm build. She looked like she was in her mid-twenties.

Helen handed her some sort of card and waved her hands in front of her. I couldn't see her face, but I imagined her mouth was keeping pace with her flying arms. If she kept it up, she might lift off of the ground.

Rita drummed her fingers on the table, a twinkle in her eye. "She's handing out business cards with a picture of the sheriff standing by the river with his shirt off. It's like she's trying to sell him like a piece of prime beef at the butcher's shop. The front lists his weight, height, eye color, and his favorite recreational activities. I bet it even includes his cholesterol level!"

"What? I can't believe it!" I exclaimed, barely holding back a burst of laughter. "I have to see one of those cards for myself!"

Bryce grinned. "She said I'm so great she needs more," he said with a chuckle.

"More what? More reasons to call the sheriff on you?" I asked, trying to keep a straight face.

"More grandkids, of course!"

Rita shook her head and rolled her eyes. "I always feel sorry for the innocent victims she chooses. Last time, she told the poor girl a story about when the sheriff was four years old and ran around the yard in a pink lace dress with peas shoved up his nose. Helen thinks the young ladies will find it endearing. I mean, I know he's a tough guy, but I don't think anyone wants to picture him in a pink dress!"

I tried to picture Sheriff Riddle as a toddler and failed miserably. He was tall, muscled, handsome, and seemed to wear a permanent scowl. The kind of man who drew the attention of the women in the room. Of course, our main interaction had been over a plastic bag full of body parts, so that wasn't likely a fair judgment.

Rita shifted in her seat. "I suspect it's the reason his clothes are always pressed and perfect and very manly. Honestly, I don't know how he puts up with her shenanigans. Anyway, what were we talking about?"

I rolled my eyes. "We were talking about Sheriff Riddle with his shirt off, next to a river, looking hunky, and the fact his mother is handing out marketing flyers to find him a wife." I thought I had problems. "I really would like to get in front of Lily," I added, scanning the room to look for her.

"What benefit is that?" Bryce asked, a hint of amusement in his voice.

"Because today, after work, I went over to visit the Hobo Hotels like I said I would. I met a guy dressed in three hats and three jackets," I explained.

Bryce smiled. "You mean Three Hats. He's been hanging out in our area for a long time. My dad knows him well because he stands on the side of Main Street and spontaneously walks out in front of cars. Drivers have to swerve to avoid hitting him. People get really annoyed and call the sheriff," Bryce added, chuckling.

"Wow. Interesting character. I asked him about the makeshift home I saw up on the hogback, and he said the stuff probably belonged to somebody named Kevin Jankins."

"Kevin?" Bryce raised his eyebrows. "Kevin disappeared three years ago. We figured he left the state. I've liked his sister, Sydney, since I was sixteen, but she fell in love with a jerk from New York named Matt Forrester. Matt is twenty-three and treats her like crap." Bryce raised his arms in the air and thrashed them around. "The girls here often fall for the transients who come to the area to ski and bike. The losers never put their relationship with the girl first, which is apparently attractive to chicks who have been stuck in these small towns all of their lives. She never talks about Kevin anymore. In fact, no one in the family does. I wonder if they knew he lived right under their noses?"

"What happened to this guy Matt?" I asked.

Helen returned from the bar and sat down at the table.

Bryce stood from his chair and paced around the table. "I don't know. I figured he got tired of the area like the rest of them and moved on. Either he became bored, or he ran out of his trust fund money and had to go back home to hit his family up for more. I heard rumors that when he drank, he became verbally and physically abusive to Sydney. She never told me herself, of course, or she knew I would kill him. I saw a bruise, once, on the side of her left eye. She claimed she got hit by her partner doing a stunt, but I didn't buy her lie. I mean, who gets hit by their partner during a cheerleading stunt? Sounds like a cover up to me."

"A stunt? What kind of stunt?" I asked, intrigued.

Helen leaned in. "She's the head cheerleader at Shotgun High School. They do stunts like tossing the girls up in the air and letting them flip around and catch them. It's like a human game of hot potato, but with more flips and less potatoes."

Bryce chuckled, then narrowed his eyes and clenched his jaw. "All of the close contact with her male partner made Matt jealous. I heard him screaming at her in the school parking lot, once. He was a real piece of work."

"Sounds like a real catch, that Matt," I said, sarcasm dripping from my words.

Rita and Helen stared at Bryce as he talked and missed the sound of the alarm buzz signaling the start of Bingo.

Bryce stopped pacing. "Lily's headed for the stairs!"

I felt a firm, stinging slap on my back.

Rita grabbed the armrests of her chair. "Go! Go! Ally!"

10

I leapt from my seat with the agility of a gazelle, snatching as many purses as my arms could hold. I dashed halfway across the room, leaving a trail of stunned onlookers in my wake. Suddenly, I heard a commotion behind me and turned to see Rita tangled up in chairs like a human pretzel and Helen struggling to rise from hers.

But Bryce, ever the gentleman, rushed to Rita's aid. "Go, Ally!" he shouted, giving me the green light to make my escape.

Lily, a woman in her early fifties with hair that looked like a blonde and gray ombre, shot me a glare that could have melted steel. Despite her fit physique, I assessed her threat level as low. But I knew one thing for sure, that woman could nag like a pro.

"You can't save so many tables by yourself!" she sneered.

But before I could respond, I felt a warm, moist breath on my neck and turned to see Rita, who was now bent over and grabbing her knees. "You know darn well she can. She did her part to help out old ladies in need." Rita shot a side-eye at Lily's pink pumps. "Maybe you should wear more sensible shoes."

Lily huffed in disapproval. "You guys hired a ringer! You're getting pretty desperate."

Rita grinned widely and draped her jacket over the back of a chair. "We didn't hire her. The insurance company did. She's our physical therapist. Bingo can be very therapeutic. Especially from the front row. Bryce, take Ally with you and get two cards for me. Make 'em good ones. I feel like I am gonna win today!"

I followed Bryce over to the window where the cards were sold.

Bryce greeted the woman behind the counter. "This is Ally. She's buying two cards for Rita, two for me and two for my grandma." He turned to me. "I can't actually buy the cards since I am not eighteen. How many do you want for yourself?"

Stepping closer to the counter, I handed the lady cash. "Maybe I'll get four cards to increase my odds." While we waited for our change, I took the opportunity to question Bryce alone. "So, what do you think about this whole Sydney and Kevin thing?"

Bryce scratched his head. "I don't know. Sydney and Kevin have always been really close. Surprisingly, she stopped talking about him at some point. I figured she couldn't handle how much she missed him. Maybe she quit because she didn't want me asking too many questions and finding out the truth."

With Bryce next to me, I walked back toward the table. "Do you think you could have a conversation with her and get some information? I would really like to know more about when he moved out of the cave he lived in and why."

"I'll talk to her. I'll have to figure out a gentle way to approach the subject. I don't want her to stop confiding in me." Bryce stopped abruptly and faced me with a frown. "I hope the body parts didn't belong to Kevin. I don't think Sydney could handle losing him twice."

"Come on, you guys!" Helen shouted from across the room. "Frank is ping-ponging up the stairs right now! He'll be ready to start any time." She sat on the edge of her chair, leaning forward as if ready to sprint from starting blocks.

Bryce joined me as I sat down with the girls.

Frank stumbled up to the front of the room. He spun the basket. The clicking sound of the balls bouncing around cued the players in the room to quiet down. "I twentyeven," he announced with a grin, before adding "Looks like we're in for a killer game of bingo today folks! Watch out for the Wrim Geaper, he's been known to be a lucky nummer!"

I looked over at Bryce, already lost. "What did he say?"

"I-twenty-seven. You'll get used to his slur. Developing the skill takes a while."

I noticed a smirk on his face. Quickly scanning my four cards, I stamped the number twenty-seven. Feeling like a pro, I sat on the edge of my seat, relaxed my shoulders and waited for the next number. *Maybe I can actually win!*

"G-fitty-two," Frank announced.

A buzz of voices broke out across the room, followed by dead silence.

Straining my neck, I looked at Helen's cards to see what number she covered. By the time I finally figured it out, Frank gave the next number.

"O-semamay-five."

Quickly falling behind, I began getting frustrated. I looked sideways and saw Helen, Rita, and Bryce laughing and grabbing at their stomachs.

"Now you know why we only play two cards." Helen laughed. "With Frank slurring his words, it's like trying to understand a drunk parrot."

Rita leaned forward, turning her head to the side. "We figured you wouldn't really appreciate the feedback unless you experienced the frustration firsthand. Plus, why would we miss an opportunity to watch the new girl squirm? If we give you too much information right off, you might win with beginner's luck. Tonight's pot is fifty-four bucks. This one is mine."

I straightened out my cards. The buzz of voices quieted again. "I thought people in small towns are supposed to be nicer."

"Only on Sundays. When God is more likely to be watching," Helen said.

"O-semumy-semum," Frank roared.

"O-seventy-seven," Bryce repeated.

For the rest of the game, Bryce repeated the numbers after Frank announced them. His doing so helped me to survive the game. Apparently, he understood "drunk slur" very well.

"BINGO!" Rita screamed.

Turning my head slightly, I jumped up from my seat in a fighter's stance, my heart racing in my chest. Embarrassed, I looked around and silently sat down.

Lily stood and pointed at Rita. "She cheated," yelled Lily. "She has the kid translating for her. It's not fair!"

"You could bring Sydney to help you next time," Bryce said.

He instantly frowned and I guessed the look meant he figured being sassy wasn't a good idea, since he might end up on the bad side of his potential mother-in-law.

"Oh, and I'm sure you would love having her here!" Lily snapped. "You've had a crush on my daughter for years. Come to think of it, I just might bring her. You'll be so distracted; Helen and Rita will lose." She plopped down in her chair, her chin lowered to her chest and her lips pursed.

Players began to rise from their tables and disperse to the bathroom and to refill their snacks.

I grabbed Helen and Rita and went over to the snack counter. "Let's leave those two alone and see if Bryce can squeeze any information out of her like a tube of toothpaste." I stood up in the front corner so I could still hear them but pretend to be having a deep conversation.

Bryce took the hint and turned to face Lily. "Lily, you and I have known each other since Syd and I were kids. You know, I have liked your daughter for a long time, but, apparently, I am not enough of a jerk. She was too good for a guy like Matt. He treated her like a doormat. Aren't you able to see what their relationship did to her?"

Lily scooted forward in her chair. "I can't believe I am going to tell you this, but I never really liked him. Sydney hasn't paid attention to my opinion for years. I always suspected he abused her, but she never let me in her room. At this age, teenage girls want their privacy, and you are a horrible mom if you violate their space. She had a dark area on the side of her left eye once, and I asked her about it. She said the bruise happened when her cheerleading partner hit her, but I never believed her. I was so happy when he left town. Since I didn't have any solid proof, I never told anyone."

Bryce looked down at the floor. "I saw a bruise, too, and she gave me the same excuse. I know he hit her. She was so blindly in love, she let him get away with it. Do you know what happened to him or where he went?"

As players returned from the bathrooms and snack bar, the noise level in the room increased. Rita, Helen, and I leaned in closer, our shoulders pressed firmly against each other like three musketeers.

Lily looked around the room before speaking. "I'm just happy he left. When I told Don about the bruise, he said he was going to look into it. I don't know what he ended up doing. Matt probably ran out of his trust money and ran back to his mommy and daddy. Either way, he's gone. I never asked Sydney about his disappearance. She began hanging around the house more and spending time with us, and I didn't want to rock the boat."

"Do you ever hear from Kevin anymore?" Bryce asked.

"Kevin? I don't even have any idea where he is." Lily looked down at her lap and frowned.

Bryce put a hand on her shoulder. "It must be hard to not be in contact with him."

"No mother likes to lose contact with her children. So much bad blood exists between Kevin and his dad. I don't bring the subject up anymore because Don gets so angry. I miss Kevin a lot." Her voice faded with the statement.

---

11

*F*rank staggered up to the front, huffing and puffing like a steam engine on its last leg.

"Looks like someone had a little too much of the sauce," Helen quipped, wrinkling her nose at the smell of Frank's whiskey breath. But Helen didn't let that stop her from winning the cash pot of the night as we played nine more games of Bingo.

As we were leaving, Lily mentioned bringing Sydney next time to distract Bryce. Helen smiled slyly, "Between Bryce's ears and Ally's fast legs, I would still have the advantage."

When I arrived home, the contrast of the silence to the noise of the Bingo Hall was like night and day. But my peaceful moment was abruptly interrupted by the sound of my front door slamming shut.

It was Rita, Helen, and Bryce. "Let's discuss the new intel we gathered," Rita said, with a twinkle in her eye.

Helen turned to Bryce, "You need to take a look at your dad's computer so we can figure out the results of the DNA test."

Bryce's forehead wrinkled in confusion. "But he's prob- ably at home. How can I get the information without getting caught?"

I gasped in shock, "Helen, you're encouraging a minor to commit a crime!"

But Helen just laughed. "He's been doing things like this for me since he was a boy. He's a pro by now."

Rita drummed her fingers on her chin, "We need to create a distraction."

Helen whipped out her phone and sent a text to the sheriff, claiming she saw three kids outside the high school with spray paint.

I shook my head in disbelief, "Wow, it took you three seconds to come up with that lie. You're impressive! Remind me not to mess with you."

Helen grinned and rubbed her hands together, "When your son is the sheriff, you think of a lot of ideas from the stories he tells you. Plus, the relationship requires having an arsenal of lies to convince him to do what you want. I dealt with his stubborn father for years and learned ways to make him do what I needed at the time. Turns out, the skill works on my pigheaded son, too."

I turned to Bryce, "I'm not sure you should let these two talk you into..."

But before I could finish, Helen interrupted, "Head over to your house and wait for your dad to leave. Find the DNA results and meet us back here. Leave your dad a message to say you are hanging with me so he doesn't come looking for you."

Bryce moved towards the door, "Will do. The search shouldn't take me more than fifteen minutes after he leaves. This is not the first time I've looked at forensic data."

Helen exclaimed, "That's my boy!"

Helen counted her money while I watched, her stack of

all ones reeking of an earthy, dirty smell of frequently handled cash. I thought about making a crack about her earning stripper's wages, but decided against it. I wasn't sure if our relationship had gotten to that level of teasing yet.

"I don't suppose you have any beer?" Helen asked, "I think better with beer."

"Aren't you on blood thinners after your surgery?" I asked, trying to hide my smirk.

Helen fanned out the dollar bills, "Dr. Dalton took me off those days ago. I'm in the clear."

I went to the kitchen and came back with three beers and two mugs.

"We don't need mugs. We drink our beers the old-fashioned way," Rita said, as she chugged her beer straight from the bottle. "Did you two see the look on Lily's face when Bryce asked if she knew Kevin's whereabouts?"

The popping sound of releasing the cap, combined with the fresh smell of hops, made my mouth water. "Yeah. She definitely lied. Maybe she doesn't want her husband and daughter to know she has been in contact with him. Do you think Lily gave him money to survive?"

"Oh, I don't think so," Helen said. "Her husband keeps close track of their finances. I've heard him give her a hard time for spending too much money on shoes."

"Don't all husbands give their wives a hard time about buying shoes?" Rita asked, as she kicked off her heels, "My feet are killing me."

"Exactly why I don't have one," I said, secretly wondering if Dr. Dalton would care about how his wife spent their money.

"Amen to that sista." Rita raised her bottle to clink with mine.

"What happened between Kevin and his dad that was

bad enough to make him live in a cave?" I asked, as I took a swig of my beer.

Helen replaced the rubber band around stack of cash, "Kevin's best friend from high school was caught with a large amount of pot. They busted him on intent to distribute. The incident happened before Colorado made buying marijuana legal. Kevin swore his friend was framed by a few guys from his old football team with a vendetta. His dad didn't believe him and did such an effective job in court proving his guilt that Kevin's buddy went to prison. The whole situation caused the demise of Kevin's relationship with his dad. He left the house and never came back."

"I guess having a powerful attorney for a dad can have its drawbacks. Did his mom try to stop him?" I asked.

Bryce came bounding through the front entrance, his face red from running. The door hit the stopper with a loud thud. "I got the results, and you won't believe who the body parts belong to."

"Well, don't make us wait any longer," Helen said, as she leaned in eagerly.

Bryce placed his hands on his knees, breathing rapidly. "Matt Forrester! Can you believe it? Matt Forrester. Turns out he didn't head home to ask for more money from his parents, after all. Wouldn't you think his parents would be looking for him, since they haven't heard from him in a month?"

Rita shook her head, "A lot of the time, the parents of kids like Matt are busy living their own lives. They don't expect to hear from their kids unless something is wrong or their son needs more money."

"Who do you think killed him?" Bryce asked, his eyes wide and mouth open. "I mean, I can think of a lot of people who probably wanted him dead, including myself." He paused, looking horrified, "I mean, I wouldn't actually kill anyone. And to cut his body into pieces? Taking such a drastic step requires a serial killer mentality."

One of my shoulders lifted as I tipped my head to the side. "Not necessarily. Mutilating someone's body takes a person with enough hatred for the victim that he wants to make a statement by breaking he or she down to the smallest parts. The act is a way to literally make the murder victim smaller than the people he dominated."

"How do you know so much about the mindset of killers?" Bryce asked, looking at me with a mix of suspicion and intrigue.

I took a drink of my beer to buy more time to think. The fizz of the carbonation bubbled on my tongue. "Let's just say I've been watching a lot of true crime shows and reading a lot of Agatha Christie novels. The subject fascinates me."

Bryce paced the floor. "Oh, that's comforting. Anyway, I think the first person my dad will consider a suspect is Sydney. I can't let her take the blame for what happened. No way she would do something like kill a person. The other two people with motive are her dad and mom, since someone was harming their daughter. You guys have to help me find the real killer before my dad goes after Sydney or her parents."

"Spoken like the true son of a sheriff," Rita said, with a chuckle. "Sydney might have wanted him to stop hurting her, but she wouldn't have wanted him dead."

I nodded. "Cutting up his body doesn't fit the M. O. of an abuse victim. Even though they have a certain hatred for the person, they still have a certain respect for them. The pieces don't fit together. But you are right, Sheriff Riddle will probably consider her first and her dad second. Bryce, why don't you ask her to go on a hike with us tomorrow? I can ask questions. Maybe we can find out what she knows, if anything."

Bryce wrung his hands. "Ok. But I've loved this girl for three years. Promise me you won't scare her off."

"I promise. I'll come straight to your house after work tomorrow. We'll hike the same hogback I did yesterday so we can see her reaction as we go past the place where Kevin stayed. I have a feeling she might know more than her mom realizes."

Bryce plopped down in a chair, looking exhausted from all of the excitement. "Okay. I'm heading home. This has been a lot to take in. I can't believe things like this are happening in my town. I thought things like this only happen in big cities."

"That's what I thought, too," I admitted. "I would have never guessed a Podunk Mountain town could be so exciting."

12

After Bryce left my house, Rita and Helen sat on the couch with their heads together, whispering like a couple of old hens plotting to steal a prized rooster from the farmer next door.

"Just what are you two plotting?" I asked, trying to keep a straight face.

"We're talking about who might want to kill Matt Forrester and why," Helen said with narrowed eyes. "We didn't really know him well. Those kinds of kids come and go so often that getting to know them is a waste of time. Sydney had motive, but for that matter, so did Bruce, her dad. Matt hurt his daughter."

Grabbing a notepad, I left on the coffee table; I wrote down a list of suspects. "Like I said, I don't think Sydney is the murderer, but I wonder where her brother, Kevin, disappeared to. If they were as close as Bryce said, the timing of his disappearance is a little too coincidental."

"Wow, I didn't think of Kevin," Rita remarked. "He's the perfect person to commit the crime. No one even knew he lived on the mountain, except maybe Sydney and the other homeless guys. What I was told is there is a code amongst the homeless demanding they protect each other as a means of survival. If the guy you spoke to said he hasn't seen him for a month, the timeline makes sense."

Helen drummed her fingers on her knee. "We have to help Bryce. He'll be devastated if Sydney goes down for any part in this."

My fingers rubbed my dry eyes. "All right. Tomorrow, Bryce and I will go on a hike with Sydney and gather more intel. Helen, you see if you can determine if they found any prints on the bags. We'll meet up tomorrow, after our hike. Watch your backs." I don't need anyone else hunting me. "As we get closer to this, we put ourselves under the spotlight for whoever did kill Matt. If Kevin plotted this whole thing out the way he did, including chopping up body parts, he might have been more affected by his falling out with his dad than people thought."

Helen and Rita looked at each other.

"Kevin is a nice kid," Helen said. "I can't believe he would do something like this in the first place. Killing someone to protect his sister makes sense but there's no way he has a serial killer mentality? He would have to have changed a lot from the kid I knew."

"Being kicked out of the family can do that to someone," I said. "Add to the picture the need to protect someone you care about, being homeless, and sleeping under a tree? The whole thing seems like a recipe for changing a person's personality. Drive safely. I'll see you two tomorrow."

After they left, I brewed a cup of steaming hot peppermint tea and grabbed my laptop. I spent time checking out my scheduled patients for the next day. As I inhaled the comforting scent of peppermint, the warm liquid travelled down my throat and relaxed my body. I found an email from

Ethel Bruner, cancelling her two-thirty appointment, so my afternoon schedule cleared out.

I added more notes about the information we gathered, in my notebook, so I could organize the scene in my head. Taking notes was a technique I used in the past to plan my missions. Of course, I hid the information immediately so no one had access to sensitive intel if they entered the house.

After work the next day, I rushed home and changed into my hiking clothes. I walked over to Bryce's house and found him and Sydney, a pretty young girl with long blonde hair, waiting on the front porch. "Beautiful day for a hike!" I commented.

"Sure is," Bryce said. "Ally, this is Sydney."

Sydney stood to shake my hand.

Her grip was firm, her skin soft. "Hey, Sydney. Nice to meet you. I've heard so much about you."

Bryce gazed back and forth between Sydney and I.

She smiled. "Hopefully, nice things. When you are the head cheerleader in a small town, people don't always find nice things to say."

"Well, I don't know about those petty people, but this one seems to think you are pretty great." I tilted my head towards Bryce, who blushed like a schoolboy.

Bryce looked down, slowly shaking his head. "Yeah, I think we should start the hike before you say something really embarrassing."

"Chicken. Let's go," I said. I winked at Sydney. At the trailhead, I steeled myself for the quick ascent. The muscles in my legs tightened automatically with the memory of the previous hike. The people responsible for designing the trail did not care much about allowing for a warm up. I tried to control my breathing as my lungs strained so I didn't look like the old city lady hiking with the kids.

"So, what brought you to our area?" Sydney asked.

Stopping, I took a drink of my water bottle so I didn't have to talk and walk up the steep hill at the same time. I could run for miles in the desert, but this mountain crap made for a whole new challenge. Scanning the mountain, I saw a young man, about twenty years old, wide shoulders and bulging belly, staring at us.

When he noticed me looking at him, he turned and walked away.

Returning my attention to Sydney, I answered her question. "I needed a change, and Mountain Tops Home Health Agency offered me a job. I work as a physical therapist."

Sydney put one foot up on a rock. "Oh, you must love your work. I am considering working in the physical therapy field. What made you pick the career?"

"After my mom got sick when I was a girl, I spent time taking care of my her," I explained. "I decided I would probably be good at helping people function better, since I spent most of my life being a caregiver. Physical therapy is a great way to assist people with improving their lives. You should research the job. It can be really rewarding."

Sydney started walking again. "I just might. First, I have to find a way out of this town and go to college."

Climbing over a large boulder, I crested the top of the mountain. The trail veered off in two directions. I didn't notice the two choices the last time I hiked the same path. I was probably too busy watching for dangerous animals.

Sydney quickly took the lead and veered to the left.

I walked briskly to pull in front of her. "If you don't mind, I would like to go down this path." I pointed to the other option. "I went down the other trail last time and wanted to try something different, you know shake things up a bit, maybe find a hidden treasure or discover a secret passage to a mysterious cave. Who knows what adventures await us on this path?" I said with a chuckle.

She narrowed her eyes but agreed with my request.

I walked slightly downhill where the path wound back and forth across the mountain. My foot slipped on some loose shale, causing me to quickly adjust my step to catch myself. A sharp pain shot across my lower back. I slowed, knowing the tree where Kevin stayed stood just around the next switchback. As I approached the tree, I looked over my shoulder and gave Bryce a slight nod.

"Hey, Syd, I saw your mom yesterday at the Bingo Hall," he said with a smirk.

Sydney scoffed. "That's not surprising. If she's not selling houses, she's at the Bingo Hall. They are the two places I know I can find her. The only time she'll be missing is when she's playing Bingo and winning big bucks"

Bryce continued. "She and I talked about Kevin. She said she hasn't spoken to him in quite some time."

Sydney exhaled. "She would never admit to seeing him, even if she did speak to him. She's afraid to make my dad start lecturing again about the requirements of his job. She still blames my dad. We both do."

I pivoted to face Sydney. "What about you? Do you have any idea where he is?"

Sydney stopped walking. "The truth is, Kevin and I have kept in touch the entire time he's been gone from the house. That is, until about a month ago. I am really worried about him and don't know what to do. I can't tell my parents, for obvious reasons. I didn't have anyone to talk to about my dilemma because I feared the people in town would start gossiping, like they always do. And let's face it, they're worse than a group of old ladies at a knitting club." She walked a few steps and came to a stop directly in front of the tree with the cave. "This is where Kevin stayed." Sydney's eyes welled with tears.

"Don't worry Syd, we'll find him, and maybe he'll have a good explanation for his disappearance, like he's been living the life of a hermit and writing the next great American novel or something." I said trying to lighten the mood.

Sydney smiled through her tears. "That would be nice, but I have a feeling it's not going to be that simple."

We stood there for a moment, taking in the surroundings and contemplating what could have happened to Kevin. As we walked away, I couldn't help but feel a sense of unease, like something sinister was lurking just out of sight.

13

*B*ryce leaned over and took a whiff of the cave. "Kevin lived here? But how did he survive living in this dumpster of a place? It smells like a compost pile and a skunk's love child had a baby."

Sydney tiptoed to the other side of the cave. "I brought him food and money, without my parents knowing. He worked jobs when he could, up-valley, where no one knew him or our family. He made friends with the other homeless people. They protected each other. When he disappeared, I asked his friends, but no one had seen him. I have been worried sick."

"Syd, I think we should talk," Bryce said. "Let's head down the mountain to the rock bench." He led the way to an opening where the trail designers made a rock bench over-looking the view of the town.

I sat on the cold, hard surface and drank water.

Bryce spoke first. "Syd, did you hear about the bags we found at Ally's place containing cut-up body parts?"

Judging by the dropped jaw, I knew she hadn't heard

anything. I knew hearing about a dead body in bags would heighten her concern over her brother's disappearance. I broke into the conversation quickly. "Syd, we found out, last night, the body parts belonged to Matt Forrester. He was a real piece of work."

Her shoulders slumped and her chin dropped. "I figured he got tired of me and went back home." Tears formed in her eyes again.

Bryce put his hand gently on her shoulder. "Syd, Matt was an asshole. He never treated you like you deserve, unless you like being treated like a doormat."

Sydney turned toward Bryce. "I just wasn't like the girls he dated back in New York. I tried to be everything he wanted."

Bryce wrapped her in his arms. "You're perfect, just the way you are. He couldn't see how great you are because, most of the time, he was too busy being high as a kite. Your mom and I know he hit you."

Sydney looked down at the ground and shook her head. "Only once. I made him mad when he said he didn't like my cheerleading partner touching me. I argued with him. I should have just let his comments go."

Bryce shook his head, gritted his teeth and pinched his eyes together. "No, you shouldn't have. If I'd been there, I would have beat the crap out of him. I would have let him know hitting women is a bad decision, like a public service announcement"

I paused for a minute, taking time to think. The chance of Sydney retaliating against Matt was slim. She'd likely talk someone else into executing a murder than do the job herself.

Sydney grabbed Bryce's hand. "You didn't kill Matt, did you?"

Bryce yanked his hand away. "What? Me? Of course not. I wanted him to leave you alone, but I would never do something so crazy. I could never hurt anyone, especially not kill them. I just really didn't like the guy. You don't think of me as someone capable of committing murder, do you?"

Sydney shook her head, a single tear running down her cheek. "No. I'm just so shocked and confused." She paused and then gasped. "Oh no! You don't think Kevin had anything to do with Matt's murder, do you?"

"Did he know how Matt treated you?" I inquired.

Sydney's eyes met mine. "I told him about some of our fights. After the time Matt hit me, I hiked up the mountain to talk to Kevin. I needed my brother to make me feel better. I lied about how the situation happened, but I knew he didn't believe me."

"Then I think this makes your brother officially a suspect," I said with a frown. "

Sydney's face turned pale with shock and fear. "I can't believe it. Kevin would never hurt anyone, let alone kill someone. He's just a little rough around the edges, but he's a good person at heart."

Bryce put a comforting arm around her shoulders. "Let's not jump to conclusions. We need to gather more information and evidence before we accuse anyone of anything. But one thing's for sure, this case just got a lot more complicated, and a lot more interesting."

Sydney stood, pacing like a caged animal. She kicked a rock, which caused a small cascade of rocks to clatter down the hillside, distracting her briefly. "Looks like I just started my own mini rock slide," she quipped. When the movement stopped, she turned and faced us. "No way! My brother is not a killer. He is a survivor. He has proven his ability to persevere over the last three years. He is my hero. Surviving the way my dad treated him takes a special kind of person."

Being mindful of her delicate state, I chose my words carefully. "Well, we need to find him before the sheriff does. His disappearance makes him look suspicious. From what I found out, no one has spoken with him in about a month. His disappearance happened about the time Matt was murdered, according to the forensic evidence."

Sydney looked down at me. "How do you know so much about forensics?"

"She reads crime novels," Bryce smirked.

"All right, smart Alec. How I know is not what matters. What does is your brother might be the most plausible suspect for Matt's murder. Figuring that out doesn't take a highly trained professional. If we don't find him, the law will."

I started my descent down the mountain.

Ignoring the burning in my thighs and calves, I did a mental checklist of the possible suspects. I planned on going over this list with the girls when I got home.

When we got back to Bryce's house, Sydney's shoulders slumped and her movements were slow.

Turning, I faced her. "Sydney, you should expect to be asked a lot of questions, yourself. You are a possible suspect in the case."

She shook her head. "Me? How could I be a suspect?"

"More than one person knows Matt abused you," I explained. "You have a motive as the battered girlfriend."

"Motive? I loved the guy. I tolerated a lot to keep him from leaving." Sydney put her face in her hands and whimpered softly.

My hand gently touched the small of her back. "What you did for him doesn't matter now. What matters is a dead body is in the morgue. Do you remember where you were or what you were doing the last time you saw him?"

"I'll never forget," Sydney recalled. "I finished cheering

at a game when he came up to me, raging because he saw me talking to my partner behind the bleachers. He thought he could convince me to leave with him, but I refused. We had a party that night at the captain of the football team's house. By the next morning, he disappeared. His apartment was cleaned out and everything."

"Did anyone go with you to his apartment?" I hoped she would say yes.

"Yes, Stacey and Heidi. I was afraid to go alone because I figured he would still be angry."

Thank goodness. "Good. Having witnesses will help, but it doesn't get you off of the hook altogether."

"I'm more worried about my brother, at this point. If something happened and he accidentally killed Matt, the mistake would ruin everything."

My hand dropped to my side. "Like I said. We have to find him. And soon."

When I got home, Beano, who had been laying on my front porch, jumped to his feet and wagged his tail like was about to get a t-bone.

Reaching down, I stroked his neck. "I guess your dad must be busy, and now I get the pleasure of your company."

Beano licked my hand, turned in three circles, and laid down. "I guess that's his way of saying 'Welcome home, boss'," I chuckled.

The smell of baked peaches and cinnamon enticed me through the front door and in search of the heavenly aroma. Taking one step into the kitchen, I saw Helen take a dish out of the oven and set it on the table.

"Dessert before dinner?" I asked. "You ladies really are rebels. Breaking all the rules of the traditional dinner order."

Helen lifted her head and smiled. "Peach crisp is the perfect way to prime your pump. Start talking."

"Only if you brought ice cream. It's considered against the rules to have peach crisp without vanilla bean ice cream," I protested.

Helen got up and walked across the room to the freezer. She pulled out a tub and brought the container to the table.

"What?" I exclaimed. "Are you a private investigator? How did you know vanilla bean is my favorite ice cream?"

She scooped a large amount and added it to the plate. "I told you already. I've raised two stubborn-headed men. I pay attention."

"My favorite cookie is white chocolate macadamia nut, just in case you need the information for our next meeting." My words sounded muffled since I had a mouth full of food. The warm cinnamon peaches and creamy vanilla ice cream combined in my mouth in perfect harmony. "It's like the dessert version of a hug," I said.

"So, what did you find out today on your hike with the kids?" Rita asked.

Chewing slowly, I waited to speak. "My suspicion is correct. Sydney did know where her brother was living. At least, up until a month ago. She took him money and food for quite some time."

"Kind of makes you sad when you think about their misfortune," Helen said. "Sydney ended up being the one to act like an adult."

"Did you tell her about the body bags?" Rita asked.

My fingers wiped the stickiness from around my mouth. "We did, and she didn't know anything about them. She seemed shocked the body belonged to Matt. She told us Kevin knew Matt abused her. She's worried Kevin could have accidentally killed him."

"Does she have any idea where he is now?" Rita asked.

I shook my head. "I told her we need to find him soon. According to my calculations, he just became the number one suspect in a murder. And I'm pretty sure that's not on his social media page."

14

*R*ita took a bite of the peach crisp and looked me in the eyes. "We can't rule out Sydney, either. Abused girlfriends have been known to fight back."

My fork made a high pitch squeak as I scraped my plate. "Her killing him doesn't fit. Besides, she has witnesses to corroborate her story who were with her at the time he disappeared. The alibi is not rock solid, but it makes her a less likely suspect. Plus, I don't think she is that good of an actor. She was genuinely surprised when we told her about Matt."

"So, how do we go about finding Sydney's brother, Kevin?" Helen asked.

"I think I will double back to the Hobo Hotels again. I found only one person there when I went. Maybe one of the other residents knows something more."

"I'm coming with you this time," Rita said. "You could use my mature skills to help coerce information out of them."

My eyebrows raised. "Mature skills? Is that what you call using the elderly card?"

Rita put her elbows on the table. "If you're good, you use what you have. Just because you are more attractive and younger doesn't mean you will get any further than I will. I can be pretty convincing, at times."

"When talking someone into risking their life while you shoot a gun, yeah, you can be convincing," I sassed. "But during the fiasco, I had to be nice because I was on the job. These guys don't work for you, so you might have to use other forms of manipulation. Maybe you should bring your cane so they feel sorry for you." Rita punched my arm using her pointy knuckles.

"Funny girl. I think I will bring the darn thing in case you try mouthing off to your elders again. Speaking of being nice to the old people, how would you like to go to the Flaming Mountain Festival tonight?"

The groan I let out was louder than I intended. "I'm afraid to ask. What is the Flaming Mountain Festival?"

Rita pushed her plate to the side. "The event happens every year. It's a festival to celebrate the firefighters who saved the town from a fire which almost engulfed all of the houses in the area. There will be live bands, booths with food, homemade goods, and local artwork. Dr. Dalton plays in a band. He will be there and I heard he's not half bad on the guitar, but don't tell him I sent you."

Choosing to ignore Rita's last comment, I pushed away from the table. "The important question is, will there be beer?"

Helen reached for her walker and stood. "It wouldn't be called a festival if they didn't have beer. The alcohol tent is the busiest one of them all. We'll be back to pick you up at six o'clock. We'll make our dinner a combination of funnel cakes, brats, and corn on a stick."

I found myself suddenly interested. "Sounds like my kind of dinner. See you at six o'clock."

Despite the fact I told myself I felt no attraction to the doctor, I ended up in my closet searching for an outfit for longer than normal. I put makeup on, which is something I rarely did. Terrorists and criminals did not care about appearance. When I finished, I examined myself in the mirror and couldn't help but think, I actually looked pretty. And who knows, maybe the good doctor will be impressed by my new look, or maybe I'll just have to use my secret weapon and spill beer on him. Only time will tell.

Beano barking distracted me from my thoughts right before my doorbell chimed. I went to the front of the house and opened the door and found Bryce smiling and fidgeting.

"I had to come and tell you really fast," he said, panting. "Syd just called me. Apparently, Kevin borrowed one of his high school friend's cell phones and texted Sydney. He asked her to meet him at the Flaming Mountain Festival. He wants to talk to her about something. They are meeting behind the stage at seven o'clock."

"He's taking a huge risk being around crowds of people. I hope he plans to be in disguise."

Bryce nodded. "Actually, he told her he would be difficult to spot. He's wearing a red, sleeveless shirt, a gray *Yes We Cannabis* ball cap, and a brown, shaggy beard to hide most of his face."

"Sometimes opportunities fall right in my lap! It's a good thing Rita and Helen are on their way to pick me up to go to the festival. We'll make sure we are conveniently located nearby. Did she say if she plans to tell him about Matt?"

He shrugged. "I think she does. First, she wants to see what he has to say. There must be some good reason he wants to meet her. He wouldn't go to such lengths to say hi. Well, I better go. She should be at my house in about fifteen minutes."

Bryce left shortly before Rita and Helen showed up in Rita's sportscar.

Beano bounded down the steps and waited patiently until the two ladies slid out of the car. He followed them to the porch and returned to his preferred spot on the floor.

Helen and Rita saw me and paused for a minute.

Lifting my chest, I took large steps toward the car. "Just drive. You need to keep your full attention on not crashing."

Rita slid into the driver's seat. "I thought you didn't care about attracting the good doctor?" Rita looked over the front seat. "You sure look good for someone who doesn't care. You're dressed to impress and ready to play."

I rolled my eyes. "I'll take your snide remark as a compliment and ask you to change the subject."

We arrived at the festival, which must have attracted most of the town. People milled about everywhere, and some danced in front of the stage. The smell of funnel cakes and kettle corn wafted through the air. The fantastic, sweet aroma started the juices flowing in my mouth.

We walked through the booths and looked at local art, jewelry, homemade soaps and lotions, handmade pottery bowls, homemade salsas, and beef jerky. One booth had hammock chairs, and I considered replacing the two rickety ones on my front porch. The stands included an entire row of various food tents selling gyros, Navajo tacos, BBQ, and, of course, funnel cakes and kettle corn.

As we walked around, I couldn't help but think this festival is a perfect place to get away with murder, or at least to sneak a peek at a suspect.

In front of the music stage, people sat in lawn chairs or on blankets. Some stood drinking beers from the large tent bordering the area.

"Do you want to hit the food first or go straight to the lagers?" Helen asked. "I brought my rolling walker to carry all of the food so we can keep our hands free for the good stuff."

"You're obviously a seasoned pro," I joked.

Helen nodded. "After you wait in line to buy tickets and show your ID, you wait in line for the beers. Next, you have to wait in line for food. If your hands are full by the time you buy the food, you might decide to skip eating. If you do, you end up getting drunk and dancing too close to the people watching the band. They don't really like when you end up in their laps. It's important you get the sequence correct."

"Why do I feel like you are talking about this woman over here?" I pointed at Rita.

"Someone has to lead the good time," Rita said. "I'm having a funnel cake first so I don't get too full on the other stuff."

I followed them over to the food stands.

Rita ordered one topped with strawberries and whipped cream. When she saw the final presentation, she smiled from ear to ear as if she had made the concoction herself. "If we share this, we'll have room in our stomachs to have Navajo tacos, brats, and corn on a stick."

The heartburn began early in my chest. "Sounds like a plan. Maybe I should have worn my leggings instead of these jeans. They would stretch better around my waist. I can tell I will need more room."

Rita licked her fingers and pulled out a handful of napkins. "We'll do some dancing to burn off the extra calories. Let's go sit in the grass and listen to music. Helen can sit on her walker."

Walking behind them, I shook my head. "Yeah, I don't dance. I would have to drink a few more beers before you could convince me to embarrass myself."

"Challenge accepted." Rita wiped her hands and mouth.

Resuming her pace, she tripped over the foot of a guy sprawled on a blanket, nearly falling in his lap.

Laughing, I glided around her. "Still working on that depth perception thing, I see. Maybe you should stick to the beer and leave the dancing to the pros."

Finding an empty spot on the grass, I helped Helen find a flat section to place her walker. Rita plopped down next to me as I sat near Helen. After tearing off a piece of funnel cake for myself, I held the plate for the other two so they could do the same. I hadn't had one since I was a kid and had forgotten how good they were. Struggling to contain myself, I attempted not to eat more than my share. By the time we finished, we all had strawberries and whipped cream covering our fingers.

As I wiped the stickiness off of my hands, I watched a unique group of women standing in a circle wearing flowers in their hair, broomstick skirts, and throwback seventies shirts. They clearly took the festival thing very seriously. Several people danced in the grassy area right in front of the stage. Busy people

watching, I didn't notice Dr. Superman's band performing on the stage.

He looked straight at me.

I smiled, feeling uncomfortable and gave a slight wave.

He nodded his head and continued playing his guitar.

Warmth coursed through my body. As I finished cleaning my hands, I noticed Rita and Helen smiling at me.

"It looks like someone has radar vision for you," Helen said. "Picking you out of the crowd didn't take him long."

"I'm ready for a beer. Do you two want one?" I got up before they answered and rushed to the beer tent. I did not want to have another conversation about their match-making attempts.

Shortly after walking away from the meddlers, the

burner phone buzzed in my pocket. Thank goodness. Maybe it's Deputy Cunningham to my rescue. I glanced around before answering: no one within ear shot. "This is Evans."

"Cindy, this is Cunningham. How's it going there?"

"I'm eating fattening food and sitting around listening to music. You better get me out of here before my body gets fat and soft. Please tell me you have good news." Easy, don't sound desperate.

"I wish I could tell you to come home, but we heard Abdul's men were spotted in Chicago asking about you. They flashed pictures of you in people's faces. Obviously, they are working their way west. I'm not happy about the news and neither is the director. Director Sanchez still thinks you are in the best location for now. We don't plan to move you any time soon. Stay out of trouble."

Cunningham hung up before I could protest.

"Well, I guess it's a good thing I'm not on a secret mission to infiltrate a terrorist group while I'm here," I thought to myself, trying to find the silver lining in the situation. "I guess I'll just have to stick to solving a murder case instead."

———

15

*D*isappointment filled every inch of my body, but I knew one thing that would make it all better...a cold beer! On my way to grab one, I stumbled upon a crowd of people gathered around a pile of freshly cut tree stumps. Being a curious cat, I made my way to the front of the crowd to see what all the fuss was about.

In the center of it all stood a young man with auburn hair, broad shoulders, and a belly that would make Santa Claus envious. He was wielding a large ax with a determined look on his face. It was then that I realized it was the same man I had spotted on the hogback when I hiked with my friends Bryce and Sydney.

I squeezed my way into the crowd next to a young mother and her child who were cheering and shouting, "Come on, Ronnie! You got this!"

"Excuse me, can you tell me what's going on here? It must be something pretty exciting for all these people to be standing around staring at a man and a pile of wood," I asked the woman.

"It's the annual wood splitting contest," she replied, "Do

you want to move up a bit so you can see better? We can slide over a little."

I shook my head, "No thanks, I'm good. I don't want to get too close in case he loses control of that ax."

The woman chuckled, "Oh, that's not happening. The man holding the maul is Ronald Riley. He's won the contest for the last three years. He's so good he could split a fly on top of a piece of wood with one eye closed."

The sound of wood splitting filled the air as I watched Ronald in amazement. I couldn't help but wonder how accurate the average person could be with such a long handle. He must have practiced for years to be good enough to win a competition using something so cumbersome.

Suddenly, a voice from behind me said, "Are you going to compete next?"

I turned abruptly to find Dr. Dalton standing there, with his usual charming smile. *How the hell did you sneak up on me again? My detective skills are slipping.* "I would make a fool of myself," I replied. "I haven't cut firewood since I was a kid. I helped my uncle once when I visited him and almost cut my foot off. Aren't you supposed to be on stage, entertaining the masses?"

Dr. Dalton smiled with a mouthful of gorgeous teeth, "We're on a break. And I'm not surprised to find you over here where things are getting cut up. Chopped things seem to be a favorite subject of yours."

Crossing my arms, I turned back toward the competition, "Very funny. But aren't you being a little hypocritical? You cut up bodies for a living. Maybe the sheriff should consider you a suspect, cutting up things like a jigsaw puzzle."

Dr. Dalton stepped in close behind me and placed his hand firmly on my shoulder, "If I needed to hide a body, I would never put the pieces in bags. I have plenty of other ways to make someone disappear without being detected."

My instincts kicked in, and I controlled the urge to yank his hand off my shoulder and twist it behind his back. But then, the musky smell of his cologne worked its magic and my body relaxed. *Take it easy, Ally. He's just having fun with you.* "Oh, that's comforting," I said with a forced laugh, "Remind me to never hang out with you alone."

Dr. Dalton grinned, "Actually, I hoped you would go to lunch with me tomorrow. They're serving prime rib at the Rock Creek Dining Company. It's so good it'll make you wanna whack a cow with an ax yourself!"

I couldn't help but chuckle at his cheesy pun.

I paused before answering, trying hard to think of an excuse. "I think I told Rita and Helen I would meet them at Helen's house to make pies.

"Pie-making day isn't until Sunday," Helen said from over my left shoulder. "We wondered why you didn't return with our beers. You've been gone for a while, and I'm parched."

"Oh, sorry. I saw all of these people gathered here and my curiosity got the best of me. I'll go and buy them now." I turned and took a step.

"She can meet you for lunch tomorrow," Helen said. "I won't be getting my bushel of apples until Saturday, so it turns out she isn't already committed."

Rotating towards Helen, I gave her a glare. "I guess I am free. What time would you like to go?" Dr. Dalton grinned wide. "I'll be at your house to pick you up at one o'clock. See you then." He gave Helen a wink before he turned and walked back towards the stage.

"Have you always been the town matchmaker, or just where I am concerned?" I asked.

"It's a lunch date. He didn't ask for your hand in marriage. Besides, you can gather some information about the body. I mean, the victim's body." Helen snorted and high-fived Rita.

Rita laughed. "Hey, at least she didn't hand you a business card with all of his private details and a picture of him half naked. I'd consider myself lucky if I were you."

"You're a great comedian, Helen. Maybe you should stick to teaching people how to bake pies." I took off walking towards the alcohol tent with Rita and Helen following behind. The sour smell of beer mixed with the pungent body odor almost made me change my mind about buying anything.

After making my purchase, I went to the Navajo taco booth and got a loaded taco. I stepped two stands down and added corn on a stick to my meal. Instead of going back to the same spot of grass I chose before, I went to a shaded spot under a tree behind the stage. A small, man-made creek ran along the road where some kids played about twenty feet away. I sat in a circle with Helen on her walker. Rita barely kept her plate from tipping as she lowered to the ground. Each of us had a different vantage point to watch for Kevin's arrival.

I took an embarrassingly large bite out of my taco, sour cream ran down my chin. As I wiped my face with the back of my hand, I saw Bryce and Sydney walk behind the stage. With my mouth too full to talk, I elbowed Rita and tilted my head towards the pair.

She nodded and kicked Helen with her foot.

"Ouch! What the hell? You really need to work on controlling your body," Helen said.

A man approached them who matched the description Kevin gave Sydney.

I leaned forward to stand. "We need to move closer so we can hear them talk."

Rita grabbed my elbow and pulled. "I got this." She

reached in her ear and adjusted her hearing aid. "If I turn up the volume on this baby, I can hear conversations twenty feet away."

Sydney moved towards Kevin, her expression changing several times. She leaned in to give him a hug, but he backed away, putting his hands out.

Rita repeated the words as she heard them. "Hi, Syd. Thanks for meeting me. How are you?"

Kevin looked around the area multiple times.

Sydney took a step back with a downturned mouth.

Rita parroted rapidly, "She wants to know where he has been. Says she's been worried sick."

Kevin pointed a finger at Bryce.

"Kevin has been in different places. He wants to know if it is safe to talk with Bryce around."

Helen and I looked at each other and shrugged as I struggled to understand Rita's fast speech. I leaned in close to Rita's ear to listen for myself. Her hearing aid made a loud screeching noise, and I sat back slightly. I could still hear the voices.

Sydney nodded. "Yeah. He knows I kept in touch with you. I needed someone to talk to after you disappeared. I was worried you joined a cult or something."

Sydney grabbed Bryce by the elbow and pulled him in closer.

Kevin took a small step back. "But he's the sheriff's son!" He shifted from one foot to another.

Bryce put his hands out. "Listen, man. I care about Sydney a lot. If she cares about you, then so do I."

Kevin looked around again briefly. "All right, let's sit down. This will take a while and I feel like I have been running for months."

The three sat in a circle.

The screams and shrieks of the children playing nearby

made hearing every detail difficult through the microphone of Rita's hearing aid.

"Where have you been?" Sydney asked.

"I found a new place to stay," Kevin answered. "It's further up-valley. Syd, I have to tell you about what happened. You can't tell anyone. That means you, too." He looked at Bryce.

Sydney put her hand on Kevin's knee. "I just want to know what happened to you."

Kevin gazed at the children playing. "Do you remember the last time you visited me? You told me Matt hit you?"

Helen leaned in, pressing on my shoulder.

"I needed to talk. I felt alone and sad." She and Bryce exchanged a sidelong glance.

"Yeah, well. The news brought out all kinds of feelings about not being close enough to protect you because of Dad. The more I thought about the crap, the angrier I got."

"What did you do, Kevin?" Sydney abruptly removed her hand from Kevin's knee.

Kevin slumped. "I spent days watching him. I saw where he went, who he visited, and how he passed his time. I wanted him alone so I could scare him into leaving town or, at least, breaking up with you. Every evening, at about six o'clock, he ran on the hogback, and I took the opportunity."

My mind raced and my heartbeat quickened, knowing that if Kevin admitted to killing Matt, Sydney's life would be thrown into a whirlwind of change. And Bryce's too, of course. Everything around us quieted as if everyone was holding their breath, waiting for the big reveal.

"One night, I waited for him and jumped out to scare him," Kevin began, a twinkle of mischief in his eye. "I wanted him to feel the same fear that I knew you felt when he hit you. But when he saw me, he started swinging. His second hit connected. He punched me in the face, and I went a little bit mad. I wanted him to pay for everything he did to you. I hit him until he begged me to stop. He kept saying he never touched you, which made me even angrier."

Sydney's eyes filled with tears. "Kevin, please tell me you didn't kill him," she pleaded.

Kevin's brows furrowed and then his eyes opened wide. "Kill him? No, of course I didn't kill him. I'm not stupid. I let him know he should never touch you again. My plan worked. I heard he left town and went back to New York. He won't hurt you anymore."

"That's the last time you saw him?" Bryce asked, slowly. "About how long ago did this happen?"

Kevin paused momentarily. "Probably about a month ago."

"Matt didn't leave town, and he isn't in New York," Sydney leaned forward "Kevin, he's dead. Someone killed him, cut his body into pieces, and put them in black trash bags. The murderer dumped them at the old Anderson house."

Kevin jumped to his feet and took a step back. "What? No way. He was alive when I left. Bloodied from when he busted me in the nose and when I split his lip, but he was alive. I swear. He apologized as I walked away. How do you know the parts belonged to him? Maybe they made a mistake."

"Dr. Dalton tested the DNA," Bryce spoke slowly, "The test results identified the body as belonging to Matt. Did you see anyone else around when the fight happened?"

"No, no one else was around, just the two of us," Kevin said, looking a little bit confused. "How did he die, and who would do such a thing?" He grabbed the sides of his head. "Oh my God, they are going to think I killed him. They probably found my blood at the scene. I'll never convince them I didn't do it. I'm one of the homeless guys now. They are always blamed for crimes they didn't commit."

Sydney put her hand on his arm. "I believe you, Kevin. I appreciate you trying to protect me. I wish the whole fight didn't happen."

I leaned forward to stand, but Rita squeezed my arm, as if letting me know to approach carefully. Kevin looked me up and down and turned to walk away.

16

"Kevin, wait! Don't go running off like a scared cat," Sydney cried. She pulled on his arm to turn him around. "This is Ally, a friend of mine who just so happens to be an amateur detective in her spare time. She found the cave where you've been hiding and knows all about our secret chats. She's the one who found the black bags and hoped to find you so we could clear your name in this murder case."

I took a step forward, trying to keep my distance from Kevin's questionable body odor. "Can I ask why you decided to disappear after the fight?"

Sydney nodded, "Yeah Kev, if you didn't kill him, why did you run like a criminal?"

Kevin threw his hands up in the air, "I swear, I didn't do it. He was still alive when I left. I knew that Matt, being the rich New Yorker he is, would call in his buddies to take me down. So, I did the smart thing and ran like a guy in a barfight."

I couldn't help but chuckle at the imagery. "The problem

is, you're now the prime suspect. If your DNA is all over the crime scene, it's not a good look for you. Do you have any idea who else might have wanted him dead?"

Kevin shook his head, "The guy was an absolute jerk. I'm sure there were plenty of people who wanted to see him suffer, but I can't think of anyone crazy enough to chop him up into pieces."

I leaned in closer, trying to keep our conversation private. "The killer had to be someone with a lot of hatred and a desire for power. Until we find out more information, it's probably best if you disappear for a while. Sydney and I are also suspects, so we need to figure out who did this before the sheriff starts digging too deep."

Kevin looked at Sydney with a frown.

Tears streamed down her face.

Kevin grabbed Sydney's hand. "It's going to be okay Syd. We've been separated before and we'll survive this too. I made you a promise when I left and I'll keep it. I'll still be in your life, you just won't see me. I love you Syd."

Sydney embraced Kevin tightly, tears streaming down her face.

Helen and Rita were also wiping away tears.

"I love you too, Kevin. Please stay safe. As soon as this is all over, we'll find a way to be together without anyone tearing us apart."

Before Kevin turned to leave, I saw tears in his eyes just as he pulled down the bill of his hat to hide his face.

"Come on Syd, let's go home," Bryce said, placing a comforting hand on her back.

I walked over to Helen and Rita, who were still wiping away their tears.

"We've got to figure out who did this, Ally," Helen said. "Those kids have suffered enough."

Bending over, I picked up the remnants of our meal, "I agree. Assuming Kevin is telling the truth. The question is, how did someone get to Matt so soon after the fight? The killer had to be someone who saw him go up the mountain. He or she could be someone who was stalking Matt and maybe had a plan to kill him. Maybe the agenda conveniently changed once Kevin started fighting with Matt."

Rita chimed in, "We need more information about the time of death and what tool the killer used to dismember the body. Things, say, a coroner would know. I wonder who might have access to such a person. Like, for example, someone who might have a date with him tomorrow?"

Stepping over to the trashcan, I emptied my hands. "Body parts in a bag is not great lunch conversation."

Helen chuckled. "You can make it work. I have faith."

"So, this is why you pushed me into this date. To investigate a murder?" Helen smacked my butt like a football player headed to the field.

Helen rubbed her hands together excitedly. "Investigating is a part of every first date. We think you and Dr. Handsome would make a great pair."

Truthfully, I already missed not being involved in solving crimes. Helping my two buddies work this case would help pass the time, until the director lets me return to D.C.

I laughed, "Well in that case, we better call it a night. Keeping up with this town is taking a lot more energy than I have. I figured I would be lonely and bored, but I have had no such feelings."

"You're in the mountains now," Helen said. "Adventure is part of the appeal."

As Rita dropped me off at my house, she said "Sleep well. We'll see you after your date tomorrow, unless the lunch lasts into the night."

I took a few steps towards my house, but then turned back towards the car. "You two really need to find a man and stop worrying about finding me one."

Helen winked, "We don't want a man in our lives. At our age, having a male around makes things too complicated. We want to live vicariously through you."

With only an early morning appointment, I had enough time to do a little shopping for something to wear on my date. According to my internet search, the only options for clothing included a large chain department store and a discount clothing store, both located in Defiance. Washington D.C. had a lot more choices, even though I rarely shopped for myself.

When I strolled in and saw the racks and racks of clothing and people milling about, I almost turned around and left. How women enjoyed this kind of thing, I'd never know. Finding my assigned target on the busy streets of D.C. seemed easy compared to selecting an outfit in this maze of racks and shelves. Maybe the tacky matching polo shirt and hiking shoes weren't so bad, after all. Oh, yeah, REAL attractive.

Exasperated, I almost gave up when I found a floral sundress on the end of a rack. Score! I'll take it. A pair of sandals and I would be out of there. I picked a simple, low-heel sandal with a tan leather strap and bolted for the registers. Who needed a personal shopper when you could just grab whatever you wanted and run like a criminal?

After getting ready, I paced the house, my heels clicking on the floor. Being alone with a man for the first time in a long time unnerved me more than being targeted by Abdul's men. My job at the agency didn't leave time for dating, which I didn't really mind. My job had always come first, and most men found the idea intimidating.

A scratch at the back door sent me instantly into high

alert. I retrieved my gun from the table, slid against the wall and looked out the closest window, assessing where the noise came from. My finger poised over the trigger.

17

_J_ found Beano waiting to be let in, scratching at the door like a detective trying to crack a case. "That's a unique way to get my attention," I said. "Next time, you should use the obvious approach and try barking. That would be less likely to get you in trouble."

Beano looked up at me with big, brown eyes, wagged his tail, and let out a bark so loud it could've woken the dead. "Wow, you're smarter than I thought," I said, and reached down to give him a pat on the back. "Come on in. Maybe you'll help to calm my nerves or scare away my problems altogether."

Beano padded across the floor, went straight to the couch, and laid down. "Maybe not," I said, sitting next to him and petting his soft fur. He had a wet and musty odor, and I sniffed my hands to see if they smelled like him. I went into the bathroom and washed them and returned to my spot on the couch. About the time the muscles in my legs relaxed, Beano jumped down and barked at a car coming up the driveway. I walked out on the front porch.

Dr. Dalton got out of his vehicle, dressed in a sports

casual outfit that hugged his lower body in a way that made me want to solve the mystery of what was underneath. "Looks like Beano has now become your watchdog," he said.

I could smell his warm, woody cologne from where I stood. *Did I remember to shave my legs? Keep it slow, Ally.* "Yeah. Since he is not around every day, I figure my house is just one on his list. You look nice."

"Thanks. You look quite impressive, yourself. I've been thinking about eating prime rib all morning. Let's go."

I filled the journey to the restaurant with comfortable, unforced small talk. Apparently, being introduced over a bag full of body parts was enough of an icebreaker for any relationship. At the restaurant, I began to slide out and saw him racing around the car to open my door. I quickly pulled my legs back in and waited. "Sorry. It's been a while. I usually do most things myself."

"It's all right. I'll have to learn to move faster." He reached for my hand and helped me out of the car.

The restaurant, an old, rustic wood building, had a free-standing fireplace perched in the middle of the room. Elk antlers hung on the walls, intermixed with pictures of local artwork. The smell of smoky prime rib made my mouth water.

The hostess walked us to a table in the center of the room.

"Do you mind if we sit over there?" I pointed to an open table in the corner.

"'Not at all. Right this way," she said, then picked our menus and water glasses off the table and led us over to the one I chose.

The other patrons noisily chatted at their tables.

I moved quickly to be the first one to choose my seat. I made a habit, during my first few days as an agent, of not sitting with my back to the entrance of a restaurant. Spotting an assailant before they saw me was paramount to my success as an agent. Hopefully, my actions went unnoticed by Dr. Dalton.

He pulled out the chair.

I sat down and helped slide the legs forward. "So, Dr. Dalton, how long have you been living here in Shotgun?"

"Please, call me Ky. I moved here after I gave up my position as the head surgeon at St. Augustine's Hospital. I wanted to live in a quieter place where I could get to know my patients on a first-name basis. Plus, I heard the prime rib here was killer."

The server approached our table to take our order.

Ky ordered us each a glass of cabernet and the prime rib.

My fiercely independent side protested silently, but I also appreciated his assertiveness.

"How do you like yours cooked?" the waitress asked. "I'll have mine medium rare with a loaded baked potato," I responded.

Ky smiled. "I knew we had a lot in common. Same for me." He handed the menus to the waitress.

Placing my hands in my lap, I opted for leading the conversation toward the investigation. "How did you end up becoming the coroner?"

Ky reclined in his chair. "Well, let's just say I'm a jack-of-all-trades kind of guy. I've had the job for the last three years. In order to qualify for the position, I did additional training in forensic death investigation methods. After being elected, I learned the coroner is the only individual who can arrest the sheriff. I didn't have any idea the position came with such power. I hope I never have to exercise my right."

Leaning in, I placed my elbows on the table. "Wow. I guess I never really thought about who has the authority to arrest the sheriff. I have been jokingly calling you Dr. Superman because you work as a doctor, coroner, play in a band, and now I find out you can arrest the sheriff. What else do you do?"

He reached across the table and put his hand on my forearm. "Hopefully, I can charm you enough to convince you to go on a second date."

Leaning back, I returned my hands to my lap. "How about we see how this one goes first? I've been a little distracted by all that has been happening with Bryce and Sydney. He found out the victim in the trash bags was Sydney's ex-boyfriend, Matt Forrester, and he is really worried about her."

Ky looked around the restaurant to see if anyone heard. "How did he find out the body parts belonged to Matt? We just received the results yesterday and haven't released the information to the public yet. Or, I guess I should ask if the sheriff knows his son has been snooping around?"

My fingertips fiddled with my napkin. "Uh, I am not sure. Maybe the sheriff told him. I'm figuring out gossip spreads really fast in this small mountain town."

Ky nodded and took a drink of his water. "For sure, but we do try to keep things quiet until we have a chance to notify the family. What is he worried about?"

"Matt physically and emotionally abused Sydney. Bryce figures she will become the primary suspect as an abused girlfriend."

"Do you think she is involved?" he asked.

I shook my head. "She doesn't fit the profile. Plus, the last time she saw him, she had witnesses. She and two of her girlfriends went over to his house to talk to him and found the house vacant."

Ky ran his fingers through his hair and leaned back. "Wow. When did you have time to gather all of this information? You sound like a trained investigator."

I waved my hand." No, I just pretend to play one on TV.

Bryce came by my house to chat. He needed someone to talk to who wouldn't be angry he told Sydney."

"Does Bryce have any guesses as to who might have wanted Matt dead?"

"Not yet. Did you come up with an estimate of the time of death?"

He paused before he answered.

I realized I might be pushing too hard.

"The results indicate the victim was killed approximately one month ago. The body had been dragged from the site of the crime and dismembered soon after. The cuts were not made by anything like a bone saw. They seem to be made by something with a sharp, heavy-duty edge. The killer had serious skill. He would need a large amount of force and accuracy to keep from crushing the bones. The cuts were surprisingly precise. The person who committed this crime made the act personal."

"Who do you think killed him?"

Before he could answer, the waitress approached with our wine.

I lifted the glass to my nose and inhaled the smell of oak, vanilla, and berries.

She waited for my nod before she left.

Ky picked up his glass and clinked his against mine. "Great timing. Having a conversation like this over lunch requires wine, or hard liquor," Ky joked.

Our prime rib arrived. I slid to the front of my seat and inhaled the smell of freshly baked potatoes and juicy steak.

"Can we change the subject?" Ky requested. "I'm bothered by combining work conversations while eating red meat. I love a good steak. I don't want to eventually have to become a vegetarian because I can't separate the two."

I laughed and picked up my knife and fork. "Sure. I understand. We had to dissect an entire human body in graduate school. I couldn't eat meat for six months after I graduated. Five hours a day, on your feet, in the dissection lab will do that to a person."

I knew exactly how much effort cutting apart bodies required, and I intended to figure out what tool was used and why. But first, I needed to enjoy this delicious steak, it's not every day you get to enjoy a prime rib like this, and I didn't want to spoil it by thinking about gruesome crime scenes.

18

---

*T*he rest of the meal, we chatted about our childhoods, families, and previous relationships, which included very few details from me. Not thinking about the homicide for a while felt nice. Answering his questions without veering too far from my cover story became a little difficult. But I didn't mind, because talking to him was like a breath of fresh air... or maybe it was just the smell of the prime rib? Either way, it was a pleasant distraction.

I finished the last sip of wine, which combined with the flavors in my mouth perfectly. "I hate to end such a nice afternoon, but I promised Helen and Rita, I would meet them at my house later. They wanted to inventory our supplies for our night of pie making."

"Why do I think you might not be telling me the whole story? Those two girls rarely do anything which doesn't involve some sort of adventure."

He paid for the meal and escorted me to the car.

I waited patiently this time, letting him open my door.

Back to the house, Helen and Rita waited in Rita's sportscar.

Noticing them when we pulled up, I hoped Ky overlooked the crazy stalkers. I let Ky walk me to the door but quickly gave him a hug, thanked him, and went inside. I didn't want to put on a show for the peepers and hear their opinions later. Unfortunately, my body didn't seem to be on the same page as my mind. The excitement left by his touch coursed through my body. I hurried back to the bathroom to take a minute before they came in. I joined them after calming down.

Helen had already poured us each a glass of wine. She handed me my glass. "We figured you had wine with the prime rib. We knew your tongue would be looser if we kept pumping more in you."

Reaching out, I took the beverage from Helen. "You guys need to work on your skills. Showing up before I got home is a little obvious. It's like you're trying to get caught!"

"We figured we would be there for you in case he got a little fresh. So, how did the date go?" Rita asked.

I sat on the couch. "Are you asking about the date or the investigation?"

Helen rubbed her hands together. "Let's hear about the investigation first. Save the juicy stuff for last."

I took a lingering sip of the wine, feeling slightly lightheaded from the first glass at the restaurant. "He verified the TOD was about one month ago. The weapon of choice, a weapon with a sharp, heavy-duty edge."

Helen pursed her lips and squinted her eyes. "First of all, TOD?"

"Time of Death, dear. I thought you two would be up on the lingo." I noticed a quick glance between the two of them.

"Apparently, we don't do as much reading as you do," Rita said. "A sharp, heavy-duty edge? The perp would have to be very strong to use that to cut through a person without mangling the body."

"Which is why Ky suggested the assailant had to have skills," I said.

Helen raised her eyebrows and smiled. "Ky? You've gotten past Dr. Superman, have you?"

I groaned. "Stay with the conversation. The person who could cut so precisely with that type of tool would have to have spent a lot of time using one. Like a professional chef or a serial killer... or maybe a serial killer chef?

Helen giggled. "Knowing the weapon wasn't a bone saw doesn't really narrow down the suspects. Do you remember me telling you about my ex-boss, Chester Riley?

"Wow," I exclaimed. "I guess we are changing subjects. But, yes, I remember. You overwhelmed me with the amount of town gossip you know. What about him?"

Helen disappeared into the kitchen.

Looking at Rita, I shrugged. The popping sound and smell of buttery goodness being cooked in the microwave answered my unspoken question.

Helen sauntered back in the room with three small bowls of popcorn. "Bryce saw a mound of dirt behind Chester's house and a hole in the ground big enough for a body. What if he had something to do with this whole thing?"

I took the bowl from Helen. "I'd like to consider all suspects, but a hole like the one he saw could have been for anything. Maybe he planned to bury his beloved pet, or something. The question is, why would Chester cut the body into parts if he planned to bury it anyway? Unless he was planning to bury a pet, but it's too big for a cat or dog, maybe he's planning to bury his ex-wife, who knows? "

Mentally, I added Chester to my ongoing list of potential

suspects. I didn't want Rita and Helen tipping our hand by talking to Chester without me.

Helen huffed. "Chester is too much of a selfish ogre to have any pets. They would probably run away, even if he did have one. He wouldn't feed them, since he would have to spend his hard-earned money on pet food. People don't generally leave a large pit in their backyard without a reason. I figure it's worth considering."

I shoved a handful of buttery popcorn in my mouth and let it melt on my tongue. "Did Chester Riley even know this kid, Matt?"

"Chester did the plumbing for the family who lived in the house where Matt rented," Helen answered. "Maybe he had some interaction with Matt when he did a job there. Plus, Sydney went to high school with Chester's son, Ronald. They've known each other for a long time. Ronald has always been somewhat of a troubled child. Chester told stories about him that made me happy I never had children."

Suddenly getting an idea, I faced her. "Helen, text Bryce and tell him to come over. He and I can go to Chester's place and take a look." I bounded up the stairs to change back into my work clothes.

When I returned, Rita bolted to her feet and fell forward into the coffee table. Bracing herself with her palms, she looked up at me. "You're not going without me. I want to see this gravesite for myself."

"You can't even control your body enough to stand up without falling over," I exclaimed. "What if you fall in?"

Bryce arrived, smelling like hay.

"How did you get here so fast?" I asked.

Bryce stretched his arms overhead. "I hung out in the Anderson's old barn, waiting for you to return from your date with the doc. I fell asleep in the rafters. Grandma

Helen's text woke me up, and it took a minute to realize I where I was."

The fact he violated my space would be a subject for later conversations. "I want you to come with Rita and me over to Chester Riley's house to show me the mound of dirt and the grave you saw."

Bryce's jaw fell open as he plopped down next to Helen on the couch. "Chester's house? Are you nuts? If he sees us, he will fire a buckshot first and ask questions later. We all know to stay away from his house. He's an asshole. Oh! Sorry, Grandma. But I guess it's worth the risk, it's not like we're going to a haunted house or something, right? It's just a little grave digging, nothing to be scared of."

Helen shrugged and picked hay out of Bryce's hair, setting the pieces on the couch next to her. "No need to be sorry. It's an accurate statement. How did you get close enough to see the gravesite several weeks ago?"

"Ronald helped me with a math assignment. I paid him twenty bucks. He's smart, but awkward around people. Most of the kids in high school thought of him as a nerd, but I didn't care. I almost failed the class. Plus, he needed the money. He still hasn't gotten a job, and he's been out of high school for a year. He just lives off of his dad's money. I think he's trying to become a mad scientist"

"Bryce, I noticed you and your dad have an ATV at your house. Does your dad let you drive the thing?" I asked.

Bryce sat back and crossed his legs. "Of course. We use his ATV to scout out places to put our cameras when we go hunting. I have to navigate so he can look through the binoculars to spot elk and deer. I'm one of the best drivers I know. And let's not forget, I'm an experienced grave digger, thanks to my dad's love for hunting"

I joined Bryce and Helen on the couch. "All right. Here's what we will do." Distracted by the pieces of hay impaling my butt, I leaned over to pluck the sharp objects from my pants. After frowning at Helen for choosing to place the hay remnants on the couch, I explained my plan. "Bryce, you'll ride to Chester's house using the ATV. I'll follow in the SUV until you can veer off road to access the back of the property. You'll need to hike the last half mile so Chester won't hear the ATV. Rita, you'll ride with me until the cut off. When everyone is in place, I'll go up to Chester's door and explain I am a physical therapist, and tell him the doctor wants him to have treatment. The distraction will provide an opportunity for Bryce and Rita to take a closer look. Rita, you take some pictures of the area with your phone. If Chester moves towards the back of the house, I'll text you. Rita, do you think you can handle the hike?"

She crossed her arms on her chest. "I ran in these mountains long before you set foot in this town, and I'll run now too, if it means getting closer to solving this murder."

I raised my eyebrows. "Yeah, but your skills aren't the same since the stroke. I don't want you to misjudge jumping over a downed tree stump and lay there like a sitting duck for Chester to capture and interrogate."

Helen looked at her watch. "I think you're giving Chester Riley too much credit. You should be concerned about how you will convince him he needs to have physical therapy. He never even goes to a doctor. He's likely to chew you up and spit you out within two minutes. Or worse, he might try to bury us all in that big hole of his"

I stood. "I'm very used to convincing old people they have problems they never thought they did. Just like I did with you. The talent comes naturally to us therapists. How will I know if Chester is home right now?"

"Are you kidding me?" Helen chuckled. "The only time he ever leaves his house is for a job. And he is done working by four o'clock and no later. He doesn't believe in the after-hours emergency plumbing concept. His attitude is: if you stop it up, you drop it in the woods until he can arrive at your house during business hours. Or if you're lucky, he'll just leave you a bill for the service that never happened."

I cringed. "Oh, what a pleasant visual. He does sound like a real winner. Let's go."

19

*H*elen insisted on driving Rita and me to Chester's house in my SUV, despite the fact she had been advised not to drive yet by Dr. Dalton. After years of working with independent women, I knew arguing would be a waste of time. Plus, I figured if anything went wrong, Helen could just blame it on her "senior moments" and we'd be off the hook.

Bryce followed in the ATV, managing to keep up with us.

Helen pulled off the road about a half mile from his house to let Rita out so she could hop on the back of the ATV.

Rita shook her finger at Bryce. "Son, you better make sure my butt stays on the back of this thing. But hurry. Those clouds are storm clouds. Things are about to get wet and noisy."

Bryce patted the seat behind him. "Don't worry, Rita. I've got you. I've never lost a passenger before. I wouldn't want to be known as the ATV driver who lost an octogenarian."

Leaning out the window, I slapped the side of the SUV. "All right, you two. Stay focused. If we all are to make it out of this in one piece, we need to stick together. Unless, of course, Helen wants to drive us into a ditch and make a great escape."

When we arrived at his house, Helen barely slowed down as she whipped the SUV partially into the driveway. She slammed on the brakes and put the vehicle in reverse, backed up a few feet, and stopped.

Turning abruptly in my seat, I glared at her. "Why did you park here? You're blocking the driveway."

Helen shrugged. "I want a decent view to watch how happy Chester is to see you. Or, more likely, how happy he is to see you leave."

"But he'll see you. He'll wonder why I brought my grandma."

Helen shoved at my shoulder. "Funny girl. Now go on. You're wasting time."

I opened the door, told her to stay in the car, and walked up the driveway. Gravel crunched under each step, announcing my arrival. Passing a blue pickup truck at the top of the driveway, I caught sight of Chester standing on the front porch with his hands on his hips.

"Mr. Riley? Mr. Chester Riley?" I travelled up the stone path connecting the driveway and porch but kept an appropriate distance so as not to irritate him. The smell of fried food came from inside the house. Chester wore a ripped pair of jean overalls with one broken strap and no shirt. His grayish-brown hair lay pasted on his head with grease.

"Yeah, I'm Chester Riley. What do you want?" He crossed his arms in front of his chest.

"My name is Ally Justice, and I am a physical therapist with Mountain Tops Home Health Agency."

"I don't give donations. Why do you people always think you are owed something?" He started to turn to go back in the house.

"Mr. Riley. Dr. Dalton wrote orders for you to have physical therapy in your home. The order says you've had some difficulty with falling."

Chester huffed and turned around. "What the hell? The only time I fall is if I drink too much. Sounds like a lot of nonsense."

I replied "Maybe, but when you have the next fall, you could break your hip. And then you'll have to start calling me 'Ally the angel of mercy' because I'll be the one coming to your rescue." A faint sound of thunder rang through the air. The storm was moving in.

Chester peered at the clouds overhead. "Are you drunk? Why would hip fractures cause an old fart to die?"

I smiled and replied "Well, Mr. Riley, if you're not careful, you might just fall and discover the answer to that question for yourself."

Chester grumbled and shook his head.

"The cause is not the hip fracture itself. People die from pneumonia or other health complications which happen when you are laid up with a hip fracture. The illness gets them most of the time."

Chester put his hands on his hips and replied "You sound like a storyteller. Even if I do fall, nothing a skinny little thing like you can do would help me. I'm more likely to crush you than to be crushed by a hip fracture." He stopped talking for a moment and tilted his head to listen to the distant sound of a roaring engine, then looked back at me. "I'd crush you like a boulder on a gnat. I have to go and see what's going on out back. Tell the doctor he'll have to drum up business with some other poor sucker."

I stepped closer to where he stood to distract him from the noise of the ATV approaching. "Sounds like a storm might be coming. Listen, I understand how you feel, but I can't tell Dr. Dalton you wouldn't work with me. He will blame me if you hurt yourself because I didn't help you. Let me just quickly send him a text to make sure he is okay with this."

I pulled out my phone, making a big deal out of finding the right number. I quickly texted Bryce to let him know Chester was moving his way.

Chester went inside.

Through the large front window, I saw him exit the back door with a shotgun.

Running around the side of the house, I witnessed Rita sprinting at full speed, just in front of Bryce, through the wooded area surrounding the house. They weaved through the trees, making good time until Rita jumped too early to clear a boulder and missed. She landed in a sagebrush.

Bryce fell on top of her. He grabbed her by the shirt and yanked her upright as a crack rang through the air from Chester's first shot. Bryce let out a grunt but kept on pulling her to her feet.

Chester lifted his shotgun to shoot a second round.

"Mr. Riley, is everything all right?" I ran up beside him.

He looked at me and groaned. "I thought you went home. No, everything's not all right. I just saw two intruders on my property. I think I got one in the backside with my first shot, but you distracted me from getting a second shot off."

Crap! I wonder which one it was. "Sorry. I worried you were hurt."

"Listen, lady. I told you. I have no problem with my balance, and I don't need your help. You can tell Dr. Dalton he is a quack and should mind his own business. Now, move off my property before I decide to use the second round on you."

I put my hands up in the air. "Take it easy. I'm going."

After I heard the sound of him cocking his gun, I backed away slowly.

Chester very clearly was done talking.

When I got back to my house, I strolled in, waving my arms around. "Whew! What is that smell? It's like someone over-seasoned the Thanksgiving turkey. Oh wait, it's just my nerves. And maybe, just maybe, next time I'll bring a bullet-proof vest instead of a stethoscope.

Bryce tended to the wounds Rita received tangling with the sagebrush. Luckily, Chester had poor aim with the shotgun and missed both of them.

"Very funny, Ally," Rita said. "Maybe, if you would have done a better job distracting the old coot, we wouldn't look or smell like this."

I leaned in to look at her wounds. "I saw you leap. Apparently, you still need more physical therapy. Your depth perception is way off. Did you hurt yourself?"

Rita sighed. "Just my pride. Before the stroke, I could do that kind of maneuver with my eyes closed. But now, I'm like a blind cat trying to catch a mouse on a slippery surface."

Sniffing the air, I crinkled my nose at the smell of the antiseptic. "Maybe you should have kept them open this time."

Rita hissed and pushed Bryce's hand away as he tried to bandage a cut on her arm. "You know, you can be a real smartass."

My shoulders lifted. "I'm just pointing out the obvious. Did you take some decent pictures? How close did you guys get?"

Other than a recently filled hole, Rita and Bryce found no evidence of foul play at Chester's house. The one Bryce saw earlier had been filled in with loose dirt. The site measured about six by four feet, which would have been big enough to hold a body. However, assuming the pit was intended for a body seemed to be a huge leap in logic.

I looked at Helen. "He did not seem happy to see me. You know your townspeople. He is not a fan of the medical profession."

Helen rolled her eyes. "Chester is not a fan of a lot of things. Neither is his son, Ronald. They argued a lot during the time I worked for him. Ronald treated him with so much disrespect, I can't believe Chester let him live there. He never could hold down a job for longer than three months, which drove Chester crazy. He wanted his son to work for his plumbing company, but Ronald wouldn't lower himself to such a demeaning job."

Bryce shook his head. "My dad can be really strict at times and hard to please, but I would never treat him the way Ronald treats Chester. I guess I am lucky. My dad is not around the house much because of his job. His being gone doesn't really bother me because I know he has to protect everyone in the town and not just me."

I slid my shoes off and sat on the couch. "You are really mature for your age, Bryce. My dad left a lot, too, when I was young. He worked for an undercover agency which required him to travel a lot. We never knew where he went or what he did because he couldn't tell us. So, I know what fending for yourself feels like."

Helen lifted her brow. "An undercover agency? Your past is pretty impressive. And probably a little scary. Sometimes the bad guys go after the agent's family. Weren't you scared?"

I propped my feet on the coffee table. "My dad had our house set up for any emergency. We had a secret underground tunnel he taught me to access. He also trained me how to fight and use a gun when I was eight years old."

Helen nodded. "I thought you knew a little too much

about crimes for a physical therapist. Even one who reads a lot of books or studies human bodies in school."

Helen made the connection, which hopefully helped cover my mistake. Talking about having a link, at all, to an undercover agency was dangerous. I wasn't sure why I let the conversation shift directions except I had sympathy for Bryce. Being a child of a tough man was difficult, and something other kids never understood.

Time to change subject. "I don't have any patients tomorrow, and I need a break from talking about dead bodies. How about taking me out in your boat and teaching me how to fish on the river? I've gone before, but I sat on the side of a lake, put a worm on a hook, and waited, thinking of things to do to keep from getting bored."

Rita grinned. "Sounds like a plan. It'll give us time to relax and maybe discuss your date with the doctor. You didn't fill us in on the details. We're dying to know if he's a catch or just a big fish story."

Helen nodded. "I'm sure the other single ladies are already wondering how the new girl in town got his attention. They have been trying for years. We'll see you tomorrow morning at ten o'clock. You can sleep in and get your beauty sleep."

I sighed. "I haven't slept in late for years. I wouldn't even know how, but I'm sure I'll figure it out. If not, I'll just catch a few winks on the boat while we're fishing."

With Abdul and Fahid hunting me, a good night's rest seemed impossible.

20

*T*he next morning, Rita and I loaded the boat in the river by ten fifteen, with Helen's walker left behind on the shore. *I hope this boat doesn't smell as bad as it looks.* The smell of stale beer, fish, and pungent moss wafted through the air.

Bryce couldn't come because he had plans to meet Sydney to go mountain biking.

Rita proved to be quite the rower, pushing us away from the shore with ease. She actually did so without falling in.

Helen, meanwhile, sat in her seat and let Rita hand her a fishing pole with a lure already on the line. She cast her line first and abruptly turned towards me. "All right, spill it. Making me wait an entire night is cruel and unusual punishment."

"I'm not giving you secret information just because you have me trapped in the middle of a river," I replied with a chuckle. "I'm a private person, and I like to keep my dating experiences away from the gossip channel. Word spreads like wildfire around here. I'm sure most of the town already knows I went on a date with Ky."

"Most likely," Rita chimed in. "If the woman sitting next to you knows, then everyone knows."

Helen attempted to kick Rita in the butt but missed. "Rita primarily does fly fishing. You can use a lure like I do. Sometimes, I just sit here and look at the scenery while Rita fishes. The view is always amazing. When you cast the line in the water, you reel at a slow, steady pace. The movement of the river does some of the work."

As I fumbled with my fishing rod, getting tangled in the line, I turned to Rita for help. "You'll have to help me too. I really don't know what I'm doing," I pleaded.

Rita set up my rod and handed it to me.

I cast my line, and as the boat tilted from side to side with the current of the river, I spread my feet wide. But as I heard movement behind me, I turned to see what was happening just as the boat swerved, pitching me into the river.

Swimming to the surface, I breathed rapidly as the cold water felt like ice daggers impaling my body. "You dumped me on purpose!" I yelled, swimming for the boat. "It's summer. Why is this water so damn cold?"

Helen chuckled. "Runoff from snowmelt. Wakes you up."

Rita shrugged. "We almost hit a boulder. I had to steer around it. Hold onto the side of the boat, and I'll help you in," she said with a grin.

Pulling on the side, I lifted my leg over the edge. My muscles burned with the effort. "Like I trust you. You'll try to—"

"Ladies!" Helen interrupted. "I just got a text from Bryce. Sydney is missing. Her dad said Chester Riley sent a text to Sydney's phone, saying he would like to discuss the prospect of selling his house."

I paused, hanging half in and half out of the water. "What does that have to do with Sydney?" I asked, confused.

Helen looked at me like I'd grown a second head. "Sydney's mother? Lily? She's a realtor? She's been training Sydney to be her assistant for the last several months. Bryce said Lily had another showing so Sydney went to Chester's by herself to start the paperwork. She's been gone for hours and isn't answering her phone or texts. Bryce called Lily, and she said she hasn't heard from her."

My legs and arms started to go numb. "Get me in the boat. I'm going over there to take a look. Why would Chester suddenly be selling his house?" I said, trying to keep the shivers out of my voice.

"He wouldn't," Rita grunted as she pulled me inside. "He's lived there his whole life. The whole thing sounds fishy."

I grimaced. "Can we not talk about fish right now? I have a feeling I'll take hours to warm up. Let's go."

Rita guided us to the shore. "You're not going alone. I'll take the back route Bryce and I took yesterday. This time, I'll drive the sports car to pull in close enough. She's a lot quieter than that ATV."

"All right. I could use a backup." Back at my house, I grabbed a towel and my nine, which I left at home when I could. I drove Rita to her house in the SUV after throwing a towel down on the seat to soak up some of the water still coming from my wet clothes.

"I'm going inside to grab my revolver," Rita said, jumping out of the car. When she returned, she climbed inside her sportscar.

I raced to Chester's house with Rita following. I parked about a half mile away and hiked the rest of the way so I didn't draw attention to my arrival. I appreciated the walk as the exercise helped to warm my body. To my surprise, the only car in the driveway was a silver sedan with metal For

Sale signs in the back seat. The blue pickup truck I saw there yesterday no longer crowded the driveway.

Peering in through the front window of the living room, I didn't see any movement. I snuck around the side of the house to look for an alternative way to enter unnoticed. Unexpectedly, a second-floor window to one of the bedrooms remained open. I sighed, seeing the window had a screen. I went around the front of the house to the other side but the windows were closed and the access to them limited.

Returning to the previous side, I considered the tree as an access to the window. Climbing up the tree, my legs and arms burned from the exertion. The contrast of going from freezing cold to sweaty and hot caused my legs to feel heavy, which made me concerned about crawling on the thin branch leading to the window. Successfully making my way to the end without the branch breaking, I leaned in to pry open the screen. The screen released from my fingertips just inside the window. The skin on the back of my calf burned as my skin scraped the windowsill when I put my leg through. Landing on the floor, I knocked a laundry basket onto its side. My ears strained, listening for any sound. The house was eerily quiet.

The window I chose belonged to Ronald's, as evidenced by posters of video game characters on the walls. A black desk with a game console sat in the corner. When I saw several pictures of Sydney on the wall in her cheerleading uniform, my eyes opened wide. None of them had Ronald in the picture, and some included newspaper clippings from football games. The display made my stomach tighten. "Looks like Ronald's got a crush on Sydney," I whispered to myself, trying to lighten the mood.

Tiptoeing quietly from room to room, I cleared the area one by one. When I arrived in the kitchen, voices could be heard from out back. I dropped on the floor and crawled over to the back window in the dining area and peered over the window sill.

Sydney sat bound and gagged next to a mound of dirt.

Ronald dug with a shovel, attempting to reopen the hole.

Finished clearing the house, I had, thus far, identified only two people in the backyard. Chester's whereabouts remained unknown. I exited through one of the bottom windows on the side of the house that enabled me to avoid climbing down the tree I used when entering.

I circled around in a wide arc, and positioned myself behind Ronald. Rita hid in the woods somewhere, but I didn't have eyes on her.

Inhaling deeply, my breathe became rhythmic, and my approach went undetected. I paused to plan my path, hoping Sydney wouldn't see or hear me coming and give my position away. I crept up to his location, avoiding crushing leaves or sticks which would give away my arrival. "Drop the shovel, Ronald," I demanded, training my gun on the back of his head.

He turned around, shovel still in hand, to face me.

"I said, drop the shovel or I'll shoot," I repeated.

21

"*R*onald stood with his legs wide, looking like a farmer ready to plow the fields. "I can't put the shovel down. I gotta make sure no one ever hurts Sydney again."

My mouth dropped as my brain registered Ronald's state of mind. This kid was clearly a few carrots short of a healthy diet. "By burying her in a grave? How is covering her with dirt preventing her from getting hurt?"

Ronald jabbed the shovel in the ground, "Apparently, judging by the fact she dated that jerk Matt, she likes to go out with guys who are mean and abusive. He controlled her and made her do things she didn't want to do. She's not even attracted to guys like me. I have worshipped her for years. I know everything about her, including what kind of shampoo she uses. It makes her smell like lavender and chamomile. I know she has trouble sleeping at night because she worries about her brother living under a tree. I know she has been going up there to take him money and food." He turned his head to look at Sydney, who looked like a deer caught in the headlights.

I sidestepped towards Sydney, keeping my eyes on Ronald. "But you have her tied up and gagged."

He shifted slightly to face me, shovel still in hand. "So I can protect her. No one else seems to care about what happens to her. Her own family lets people hurt her right under their noses. The jerk she has been seeing abused her for months and even hit her. They all just pretended not to see her fear or the bruises. Even her brother can't protect her because he's a wimp. He beat Matt up but didn't finish the job. Matt would have just charmed his way back into her life and started all over again."

I took the information in and suddenly found the pieces falling into place. "How do you know Kevin beat Matt up? Were you there?"

"I followed Matt for months, watching his habits and movements." Ronald's jaw tightened. "I waited for the right time to make my move. I got lucky when Kevin showed up on the hogback. Kevin made my job easier."

"Your job. What do you mean, your job?" I scouted the area and rushed him without hurtin' anyone.

He gripped the shovel handle, the skin on his fingers blanching. "To get rid of him. To protect Sydney. Are you even listening?"

I squeezed the hard metal of my gun. "Calm down. I am listening. I don't understand how you think protecting Sydney is your job. Does she even know how you feel about her?"

Ronald briefly looked down at Sydney. "I planned on telling her, but Matt came into town and she fell in love with him. For the life of me, I can't figure out why. He was a jerk from the very beginning. I have to protect her. She makes crappy decisions on her own."

"What did you do to him, Ronald?" I asked, instinctively keeping my voice calm and steady.

Ronald laughed, the dirt crunching under his foot as he took a step closer. "That's the best part of the story. When Kevin left, it didn't even take much to finish Matt off. The only hard part was figuring out what to do with the body. You know, I really do owe Kevin a lot. He made the task of killing Matt easy and left his own blood all over the place. It was perfect."

"But why dismember Matt's body? Why not just toss it in the river or something?"

Ronald looked and shook his head. "I needed a way to transport the body. He wasn't exactly a small guy. I'm really good with an axe, and I wasn't about to carry that huge jerk all in one piece."

"Why would you do something so stupid?" The gruff male voice made Ronald flinch.

I turned my head to see where the voice came from. As I did, I saw the flash of Ronald's shovel moments before blinding pain exploded on the side of my head. My nine flew out of my hand as I hit the ground and came to rest just out of my reach. As I removed the dirt and leaves from my mouth, I looked up to see Chester standing there, lips pursed, eyes narrowed and shaking his head slowly.

Ronald dropped the shovel. He quickly picked up my nine and pointed my own gun at me.

Damn it. Keep him talking, Ally.

Ronald rotated his head back and forth, looking between Chester and I. "I had to make the madness stop, Dad. Sydney deserves to have a person who really cares for her. Someone who would never hit her or let anything bad happen to her. I don't need you. I'm a real man and did what real men do."

Chester's expression changed from a frown to tight lips. "How could you kill someone and say you murdered them to protect Sydney? It's ridiculous!"

"You are not in the position to judge me." Ronald moved the gun back and forth, pointing at his dad and myself, like an amateur who watched too many cop shows.

Chester stepped forward, "Put the gun down, son. You're already in so much trouble. Don't add to the problem by killing these ladies."

Ronald glared at Chester, "Get back, Dad. All you have done since Mom died is stay in this stupid house all day unless you're working. And when you're here, you don't even pay attention to anything around you. It's like living with a zombie. You drink too much, and you're a real jerk when you drink. Now, step back and let me finish what I started."

Chester took a few, slow steps towards Ronald, "I can't let you--"

Ronald pulled the trigger, shooting his dad in the right shoulder.

Chester spun and hit the ground with a loud thud, like a sack of potatoes. Blood sprayed the dirt as he landed.

I squeezed the sides of my head with the palms of my hands as pain from the noise of the gun seared my brain.

"Put the gun down, now!" Rita demanded; her voice full of authority.

Ronald pivoted on his heels towards Rita, lifting his hands to point the gun.

I rolled twice on the ground and swept Ronald's knees with my right leg, like a soccer player scoring the winning goal.

He buckled over backwards, his head hitting the edge of the shovel. He lost his grip on the nine, letting the weapon drop to the ground. The shovel left a large gash in the back of his head which began bleeding immediately.

Ronald appeared to be knocked out. I leaned forward to transition to my feet, but the dizziness and pounding sensation in my head made me plop back down, like a puppet with its strings cut. The sensation of water running down my neck caused me to touch the back of my head. When I pulled my hand away, my fingers were covered in warm, sticky blood.

Rita bent over to help me stand, but I waved her off and laid there for a few moments, trying to catch my breath and calm myself as sticks and rocks poked me in the back. It was like laying on a bed of nails.

She went over and took the gag out of Sydney's mouth before squatting down and working on the knots of the rope.

I started to stand up to help Chester with his wound, but Sydney screamed, "Watch out!"

I dove for my nine and aimed for Ronald just as he swung the shovel again. I squeezed the trigger, hitting him in the leg as my back hit the ground. The shovel barely cleared the top of my head as I saw his body collapse. The movement of my neck made my head spin, and I lost my vision for a few seconds, like a cartoon character getting hit on the head.

Rita stepped cautiously over to where Ronald lay and picked up the shovel, throwing the weapon into a bush. "Are you alright?" Rita asked me. "That was damn close."

"I think so, but my head is pounding. Why don't you try to help Chester?" I crawled sluggishly to where Sydney sat, rocks impaled my hands and knees. A sound of distant sirens filled the air as I untied Sydney, my hands shaking. "Did you call for help?" I asked Rita.

How am I going to explain all of this to the director? Especially with a trip to the hospital.

---

22

*J*ust as I asked the question, a strong scent of floral perfume wafted over me. It was like someone had sprayed a whole bottle of the stuff in the air.

"'No, I did," said Lily, clumsily making her way across the backyard in her ivory high heels. "Sydney, baby, what in the world happened here?"

"I figured I could start the process," Sydney said, tears streaming down her face. "I got a text from Chester saying he might sell his house. I thought I would help you, since you already taught me how to do the paperwork."

The sound of leaves crunching and someone groaning came from Chester's direction. "I didn't text you," Chester said, sounding like he had just run a marathon.

"Ronald wanted me to go into town because he said he was out of his medications. He's on pills to control his mood. If he doesn't take them, it's like living with a bear with a toothache. His mom was much better at dealing with the mood swings than I ever have been. She was a saint."

Sydney cried harder, leaning into her mom. "When I got

here, Ronald told me he would show me around to hear my opinion on how much Chester should ask for the house. When we looked at the shed, he shoved me down and put his knee in my back. I never knew a man could be so strong. I couldn't move, no matter how hard I tried. He tied my hands behind my back. I pleaded for him to let me go, but he put a rag in my mouth. He forced me to sit by a dirt pile and then tied my legs together. I tried to scream but I couldn't."

Lily kissed Sydney on the forehead. "It'll be all right, honey. The danger is over now."

Lily turned to face Rita and me. "What are you two doing here? I suppose you had something to do with all of this," she accused.

Her tone irritated me. "Bryce and Sydney had plans to go biking today. When she didn't show up, he got worried. We had already been watching Chester's property because Bryce saw a suspicious mound of dirt. We were determining if he had anything to do with the murder of Matt Forrester."

Chester huffed. "You thought the murderer might be me?"

Rita placed a hand on his shoulder. "We just thought having a grave dug in the backyard made things a little suspicious. Turns out, we weren't far off the mark."

Chester shook his head. "I planned to use the hole as a smoke pit. I wanted to smoke some elk and deer roasts after hunting. The hole had nothing to do with burying humans." As the reality of the situation hit him, his voice faded. "I can't believe my son would do such a thing. Obviously, I failed as a father."

Lily addressed Chester. "Sometimes, our kids take their own path. No matter how hard we try to protect them, we can't always control what they do. Do you think I wanted my son to end up living as a homeless person under a tree?"

Lily turned towards Sydney. "Matt Forrester was murdered?"

Sydney slumped. "I'll explain later. You knew about Kevin? How long have you known he lived under a tree on the hogback?"

Lily gazed down at the ground frowning with her jaw clenched. "About a year. I followed you up there one time to see where you always went."

"Why didn't you tell me?" Sydney asked. "Why didn't you convince Kevin to come home? You could have saved him from living as a homeless."

Lily looked away. "Your dad would have never let him come home, honey. His reputation as the D.A. would have suffered, and he would never let anyone tarnish his good name. Plus, it's a small valley. I'm not sure people would buy homes from a woman who lets her son live in a hole on a mountain like some kind of mole person," Lily said, trying to make light of the situation.

Sydney shifted to her knees. "Reputation! What does reputation matter? He's your son!"

Just as Sydney's words hung in the air, I heard engines approaching and turned my head to find the origin of the sound.

A few minutes later, Sheriff Riddle, Bryce and two paramedics walked around the side of the house. The sheriff had his hand on his holster, surveying the scene like he was in a western movie. "You boys take a look at Chester and Ronald," he said, motioning to the paramedics. "Can someone tell me what happened here?"

Rita stepped forward. "Ronald kidnapped Sydney and planned on burying her in this pit," she said, pointing to the hole in the ground.

Bryce rushed to Sydney's side. "Syd. Is that true?" he asked, looking like he had just seen a ghost.

Sydney stood and embraced Bryce. "It's true, but let's not talk about it right now," she said, trying to comfort him.

Bryce wrapped his arms around her. "I knew Ronald was different, but I had no idea he would do something like this. I should have been here to protect you.

Sheriff Riddle took a step towards Bryce. "Son, it's my job to protect people. Not yours." He turned and addressed Rita and myself. "How did you two manage to be here and get involved in this situation?"

Being questioned by the law two times in less than a week. Way to lay low, Ally.

Rita stepped in. "Sheriff, can we focus on the fact that Ronald kidnapped Sydney and planned on burying her alive?"

The sheriff moved over to Ronald and touched his neck to find his pulse. "Good thing he is still alive. How did Ronald end up shot in the leg?"

Sydney stood, lost her balance, and hit the ground with a thud. "He tried to kill Ally with a shovel, twice. He shot his dad in the shoulder for trying to stop him. Ally shot him just before he almost hit her with the shovel the second time," Sydney said, looking like she had just been through a war.

Sheriff looked at the gun on the ground. "Whose nine-millimeter is this?"

"Mine," I said, trying to sound cool and collected. "I have a conceal and carry permit. You learn to be prepared when you live in large cities." As the exertion of talking intensified the pain, I grabbed at my head.

"Jake, you need to check this one out," Sheriff Riddle said, pointing at me as he directed one of the paramedics. "Apparently, she took a pretty good blow to the head with a shovel. "

One of the paramedics walked over and began poking around at the back of my head with a painful prodding.

Bossing me around. Telling me not to move. It was like he was trying to find my brain with a fork.

Sheriff Riddle tucked his fingers into his belt loops. "Sounds to me like you two acted as the law. Why didn't you call me when you found Sydney missing?"

"We weren't sure if it was an emergency," Helen said, rolling her walker around the side of the house. "We didn't want to waste your time. We know you are busy taking care of the whole town, which is a huge responsibility, like herding cats."

Sheriff Riddle pivoted toward his mom. "You're here, too? Maybe, if you'd contacted me, I could have prevented anyone from getting hurt."

"Now, see, you would be a little late in preventing an injury,' I explained. 'Ronald just confessed to killing Matt Forrester. With four witnesses."

The sheriff took a step back to rotate toward Sydney. "Is that true?"

Sydney looked down at the ground. "Yes. Matt hit me, one time, when he got jealous. Ronald found out about the abuse and followed him to the route where he often went running. He killed him and chopped up his body with an axe. He put the parts in black trash bags and left them on the old Anderson property. He said he did the whole thing to keep me from getting hurt."

"He had her bound and gagged and dug this hole," Rita pointed at the ground. "He would have buried her in it if we didn't get here in time."

"Lily, tell me about your role in this whole thing," Sheriff demanded.

"I came looking for Sydney. Bryce said she came here. When I walked up, I heard loud cracks of gunfire and immediately called nine-one-one. By the time I came around back, Ally had untied Sydney and Rita was helping Chester."

Sheriff Riddle ran his fingers through his hair. "All right. Ally and Chester, you both go with the paramedics to the hospital with Ronald. Lily, you take Sydney to the hospital to be checked out. Rita, you stay with me just in case I have any questions. When the rest of you are able, I'll be taking your statements, as well. This one will take some time."

Rita glided over to me and put a hand on my shoulder. "Helen and I will check on you later at the hospital. We have some questions about that move you made before you shot Ronald. Sure looked like the move of a professional. Like something out of a spy movie."

23

*D*r. Dalton greeted us as we entered the hospital and instructed us to sit in the waiting room. The smell of cleaning chemicals made my stomach turn, but I couldn't help but think it was the perfect cover up for any potential murder weapon smells. He examined Chester's shoulder first and told the nurses to prep him for surgery. Next, he assessed Ronald's leg and his head and told the nurses to stabilize him until backup arrived from a nearby hospital. Afterwards, he pulled my bandages off so he could look at my head.

Ky frowned and shook his head. "Are you the one who brought me all of this business at once? What happened to your head?"

"I got hit with a shovel... at a high rate of speed. How's Chester's shoulder?"

"He'll be okay. The bullet went straight through. The repair of his shoulder blade will take some time. But he can still use the shoulder after some therapy. Who hit you with a shovel?"

I grimaced. "Ronald Riley. I'll have to explain what happened later. My head is pounding, and I feel like I need to vomit. Can I go home now?"

He shook his head. "No way. We're running some tests, and I'll have to keep you overnight for observation. You probably have a concussion, and we need to watch for signs of intracranial hemorrhage. You're stuck with me tonight."

"I guess that's one way to convince me to stay the night with you." *Oh boy. How hard had Ronald hit me?*

"It's not exactly the way I envisioned our first sleepover," he said. He winked before he turned and strutted down the hallway.

I remained under the care of his nurses. They poked and prodded and scanned me for a while. I couldn't wait to lie down and rest.

By the time I awoke, Rita, Helen, Bryce, and Dr. Dalton surrounded my bed. Ky looked tired after a long day of taking care of everyone. They whispered about the events, but I couldn't make out the details.

I slowly opened my eyes.

"How's your head?" Ky asked. He shone a bright light in my eyes.

Squinting, I touched the bandages. "Better than I felt before. Thanks. What's everybody talking about?"

"I filled Helen, Bryce, and Dr. Dalton in on the details they missed," Rita said.

I elevated the head of my bed to talk to them but changed my mind after my head started pounding and my vision blurred. "What happened to Ronald?"

Ky pressed some buttons on the vitals monitor, which made the beeping sounds stop. "They took him to the hospital in Shale. He will have surgery on his leg and get the head wound treated. The sheriff's department in Shale has someone guarding his door."

Bryce stood with his hands on the bed rail, his mouth downturned. "I still can't believe Ronald killed Matt and cut him up. He seemed like a quiet, nerdy type of kid. I would have never pegged him as a murderer. I mean, who would have thought the quiet ones would be the ones to chop you up?"

Helen wrapped her arms around Bryce. "People do crazy things when they are obsessed with someone. Plus, Chester said Ronald had problems controlling his moods. He has been a difficult child since birth. I guess the apple really doesn't fall far from the tree."

Bryce put his head in his hands. "Maybe, but he almost buried Sydney alive. She must have been terrified. I can't even let myself think about what the experience would have been like. She'll definitely need counseling now. She needed counseling before, in order to deal with her crazy family, but now?"

"I think we could help out a little by assisting her with finding Kevin," Helen remarked. "Now that he is off the hook for Matt's murder, I think returning to town is safe. Maybe, after almost losing Sydney, his parents will reconsider and allow him to come back home. I always knew Chester as a crotchety, grumpy guy, and he and Ronald didn't get along. I never knew his son would take such a drastic turn for the worse. I mean, who knew that Ronald was just a ticking time bomb, waiting to go off?"

I shifted in bed to get more comfortable and have a better view of my visitors. "Working in home health you learn things about a family you never intended. You realize, quickly, people are a lot different in their own homes than they are out in public. Not everyone is living the same life. When I receive orders to go to someone's house, I usually do a little research first so I know what I am getting into. You just never know what goes on behind closed doors."

Ky squeezed my hand between his. "Well now, I guess I will put more thought into writing P. T. orders from now on. I would feel horrible if you ever got hurt. At the time I scribble them, I am focused on how much help the person needs to live their life. I guess it just goes to show, you can't judge a book by its cover."

I gently pulled my hand free. "I can handle myself."

Rita smiled. "You certainly proved your toughness today. I have never seen someone bounce back like that from a blow to the back of the head. I guess you're like a cat, you have nine lives and all."

I touched the thick, soft bandages on my head and grimaced. "I had to do something. He was going to shoot you."

"Remind me to take you every time I put my life in danger," Rita said.

"I have a feeling you have survived many sketchy situations all by yourself," I said.

Ky stood from the chair and assessed my vitals one more time. "I have to check on my other patients. You folks don't stay too long. My patient needs some rest." He glided out of the room.

I smiled at Rita and Helen as I realized my eyes lingered for a little too long as I watched Ky walk away.

"So, now the good doctor is gone, I have some questions," Rita said.

"Okay, shoot," I said.

Helen plopped down beside me on the bed.

As the movement reverberated through the rest of my body, I grimaced.

Helen fiddled with my covers. "Funny you should choose the word shoot, because my first question is how did you REALLY learn to shoot a gun the way you did?"

I shrugged. "I got lucky. Maybe the blow to my head helped. The impact might have improved my aim."

"I'm not buying your explanation." Rita moved her chair closer. "To develop skills like you have with a gun takes years of practice. Not to mention you know a lot about forensics, crimes and weaponry. Did you really come to our area to work as a physical therapist?"

"I did." I paused, deciding what I should say next. "The truth is, I am also an agent. My boss arranged the physical therapist job as a cover and hid me in this town until things cool off back home. He's not very happy I got involved in this case. I am supposed to be laying low."

Rita and Helen looked at each and nodded. "Why do you need someplace to hide? Is someone after you?" Rita asked.

"I ticked off a terrorist group in D. C. who runs drugs. They put a price tag on my head large enough to interest some really shady characters."

"That explains so many things," Helen said. "Given what happened today, I'm really glad you came to our area. Things could have ended a lot differently, or maybe not at all."

"Me, too," Rita said.

"I'm not quite sure I was the only one at the scene with special training," I said. "For a person who is recovering from a stroke, you have some skills, yourself. Are you trying to convince me you have the talent you do just from competing as a kid in sharpshooting competitions? Were you faking the near fall when you stumbled during target practice?"

Rita moved closer to my bed. "Well, I guess it's okay to tell you at this point. I'm retired from the FBI. I was sent to this area to work on a potential homicide and had a stroke.

The director took me off of the case but left me stationed here to do rehab. I liked the area so much, I retired."

I raised an eyebrow. "Retired from the FBI and now playing in the snow, who would have thought? I guess the mountain life agrees with you."

I never did buy the explanation about Rita being the best sharpshooter as a kid. "Helen, did you know she was an agent?"

She looked at me and signed. "I was with her when she had her stroke. She mumbled something about a case, which didn't make sense. I figured the truth out later when she recovered her ability to speak."

My body relaxed after being able to share my secret. "Well, I guess we make quite the team. Not to mention, I haven't been part of a team who turned out to be my friends ever in my career. You guys are great. I thought living in the mountains would be boring, but you have kept my life exciting the whole time I have been here"

Helen leaned in and gave me a hug. "Our pleasure. We're just glad we could add some excitement to your life."

Rita placed her hand on mine. "Anytime you need backup, you know who to call." She grinned from ear to ear. "We'll be like the three musketeers, but with less swords and more guns."

My head gently pushed into my pillow. "Thank you both. And now, I am kicking you out. My noggin' is killing me, and I really do need to rest."

Helen stood and brushed a hand on my forehead. "Okay. Get lots of rest. You never know what kind of excitement another day in the mountains will hold. Maybe next time we'll be solving a mystery involving stolen pies or a missing cat. But for now, rest up and let us know if you need anything."

As I tried to relax enough to drift off to sleep, I pondered my situation. As of yet, Abdul and his band of miscreants have not found my hiding place. I have not been attacked by vicious wild animals. And I have not died from boredom. I realized I had never felt so at home.

With my new friends by my side, this small town in the mountains had become my own little haven, full of excitement and adventure. And I couldn't wait to see what the next day would bring.

————

Ready for more? Read Shotgun Showdown next!

I'm supposed to be in hiding. The leader of a drug cartel has goons searching for me—and the price on my head is growing. My boss at the DEA wants me to sit still in Shotgun, Colorado, a quirky, podunk mountain town, so I don't end up dead.

Here I am, trying to lay low and mind my own business. Problem is, my new friends keep getting me involved in things like selling toilet artwork and overly potent peach moonshine. They threw me into a fishing tournament—my skills majorly lacking—and I hooked more than I intended. A lot more.

Another dead body, and this time I witnessed his demise. I don't know why these things keep happening when I'm around. Just lucky, I guess.

The sexy sheriff isn't happy with me. If I keep ending up in the wrong place at the wrong time, I might be the one who ends up in jail.

Guess I'd better find the killer before anyone else ends up dead. Including me.

Click here to read Shotgun Showdown **now!**

ALSO BY TRENA REDDING

A Cozy Mountain Town Mystery

Shotgun, Lies & Alibis

Shotgun Showdown

ABOUT THE AUTHOR

Trena Redding lives in the Rocky Mountains with her family, 2 dogs, 2 cats, and an adorable rabbit who wears a petite crown and reigns over the back yard. Her next cozy - another small town mystery set in Colorado - is coming soon!

Printed in Great Britain
by Amazon